Mich

Lisa 2, v1.0

```
                          .^~~^.     .7YY^
                         :J#@@@@J    Y@@B^
                      .!P&@@@@P!      77        .^~!?Y!           .:^~????~.
                   .^?P&@@@&G?:  ~JGG!     .:~7J555&@#J:  ..:^~7JYPG#&@@@&#BP57
                 ^75#@@@@#57. ^?P#@@@&P~!????!^:. .#@G55YJJG@@@@@@&GY7~^~!??!
             .!YB@@@@#P?^. .JB@@@@@@&PJ7~:   .:~!75#@@J^^!YG&@@@B?^..^75#&@@7
       .~JG&@@@@BJ~.       G@@@@#PJ~..:~?YPGPY?!7&@@# !B@@@@@@#YYPB&@@B5#@@7
   :?P&@@@@@BJ^             ?B57^.  .JB@@@@#J?JP#@@#P^ &@@@@@@@@@@&GJ!: .&B^
 ^P@@@@@@@G~              .. .  ..  ^&@@@@@@@&#GY7^.   ?#&@&#BPY7^.    .7.
:&@@@@@@@&55PGGBBB#####&&&&&&&5: .~777!~^.            .:::.
 P@@@@@&##BBGPP55YYYYJJYYY55PGBP.
  777~^:..                      .
```

Welcome to Lisa 2, v1.0.

New users log in with GUEST.

Username: Nicholas Rombes

Lisa 2, v 1.0
Nicholas Rombes
ISBN 978-1-940853-34-5

published by Calamari Archive
NY, NY
www.calamaripress.com

Sections:

I. David . . . . .

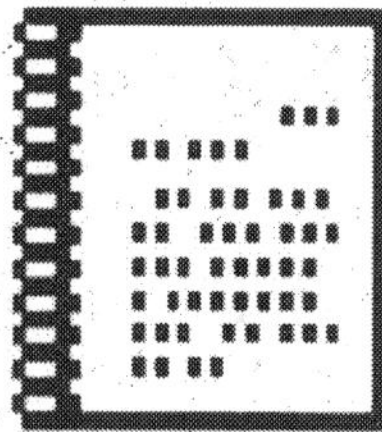

II. Lisa . . . . .

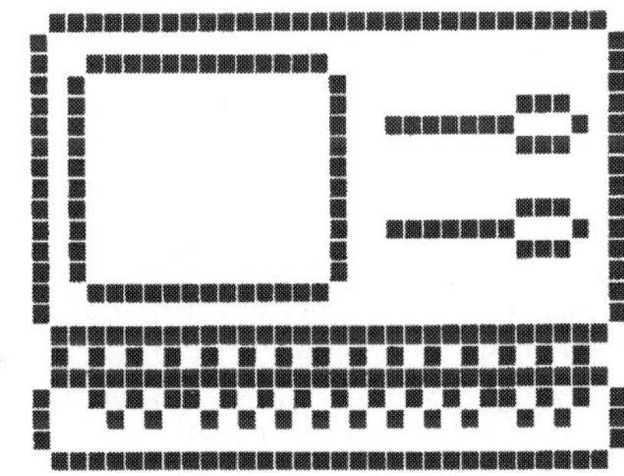

Lisa

Keyboard Layout

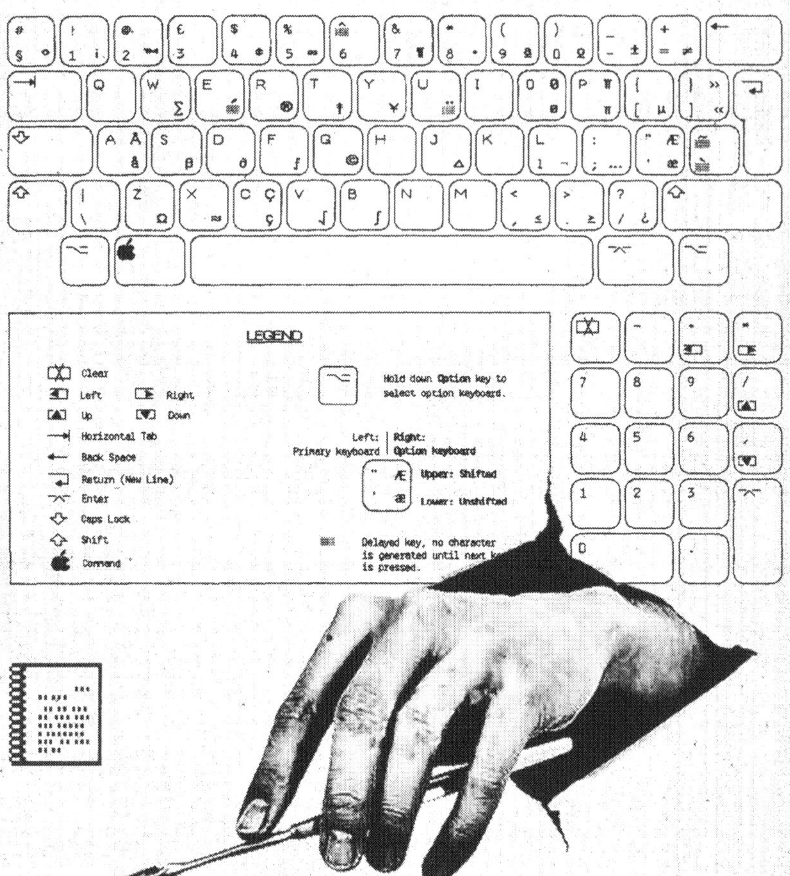

Dot Matrix Printer Self-Test

The test continues until you turn the printer off.

```
LMNOPQRSTUVWXYZ[\]^_`abcdefghijklmnopqrstuvwxyz{|}~ !"#$%&'()*+,-./0123456789:;<
MNOPQRSTUVWXYZ[\]^_`abcdefghijklmnopqrstuvwxyz{|}~ !"#$%&'()*+,-./0123456789:;<=
NOPQRSTUVWXYZ[\]^_`abcdefghijklmnopqrstuvwxyz{|}~ !"#$%&'()*+,-./0123456789:;<=>
OPQRSTUVWXYZ[\]^_`abcdefghijklmnopqrstuvwxyz{|}~ !"#$%&'()*+,-./0123456789:;<=>?
PQRSTUVWXYZ[\]^_`abcdefghijklmnopqrstuvwxyz{|}~ !"#$%&'()*+,-./0123456789:;<=>?@
QRSTUVWXYZ[\]^_`abcdefghijklmnopqrstuvwxyz{|}~ !"#$%&'()*+,-./0123456789:;<=>?@A
RSTUVWXYZ[\]^_`abcdefghijklmnopqrstuvwxyz{|}~ !"#$%&'()*+,-./0123456789:;<=>?@AB
STUVWXYZ[\]^_`abcdefghijklmnopqrstuvwxyz{|}~ !"#$%&'()*+,-./0123456789:;<=>?@ABC
TUVWXYZ[\]^_`abcdefghijklmnopqrstuvwxyz{|}~ !"#$%&'()*+,-./0123456789:;<=>?@ABCD
UVWXYZ[\]^_`abcdefghijklmnopqrstuvwxyz{|}~ !"#$%&'()*+,-./0123456789:;<=>?@ABCDE
VWXYZ[\]^_`abcdefghijklmnopqrstuvwxyz{|}~ !"#$%&'()*+,-./0123456789:;<=>?@ABCDEF
WXYZ[\]^_`abcdefghijklmnopqrstuvwxyz{|}~ !"#$%&'()*+,-./0123456789:;<=>?@ABCDEFG
XYZ[\]^_`abcdefghijklmnopqrstuvwxyz{|}~ !"#$%&'()*+,-./0123456789:;<=>?@ABCDEFGH
YZ[\]^_`abcdefghijklmnopqrstuvwxyz{|}~ !"#$%&'()*+,-./0123456789:;<=>?@ABCDEFGHI
Z[\]^_`abcdefghijklmnopqrstuvwxyz{|}~ !"#$%&'()*+,-./0123456789:;<=>?@ABCDEFGHIJ
[\]^_`abcdefghijklmnopqrstuvwxyz{|}~ !"#$%&'()*+,-./0123456789:;<=>?@ABCDEFGHIJK
\]^_`abcdefghijklmnopqrstuvwxyz{|}~ !"#$%&'()*+,-./0123456789:;<=>?@ABCDEFGHIJKL
]^_`abcdefghijklmnopqrstuvwxyz{|}~ !"#$%&'()*+,-./0123456789:;<=>?@ABCDEFGHIJKLM
```

I. David

1.

A vast red desert with shifting sand. An abandoned, moss-covered apartment building in East Germany, circa 1961, topped with enormous, wilted antennas. A movie about a possessed woman that, in turn, possesses its viewers. An endless field of white daisies. A wavy, uncertain sky that seems always about to open up. A room full of abstract art from the '50s. The paint is still wet.

I'm writing this from the other side, from all these places, and from so many more, simultaneously. Nothing disappears completely, especially me. I will tell my version in the present tense, because I live in the present tense, an eternal now. It's not my fault Lisa got entangled with Lisa 2, which then entangled me, and then Marin.

The first indication that Lisa is no longer the habitual Lisa comes in the garden, and in fact Lisa and Marin are out there now. It's not our garden, so it's interesting and new. I don't really feel at home in this unsturdy cottage but it belonged to Lisa's aunt Elle and has stayed in the family and we have come for the last five Augusts and here we are again this year. The weathered clapboard sidings must once have been painted in a dark mustard color because that is what's showing through in spots. The house is a deep red now, like the cut insides of a beet. It overlooks a large lake that, on sunny days, takes on the color of dark turquoise. In this part of northern Michigan, in the summer, all the lakes look like this. By August the black flies have gone and the water is warm. The house (Lisa calls it a cottage, but it's a house) sits on a sandy bluff that runs down to the water, and from the narrow, tilted attic window you can see beyond the lake to the little town with its creepy, white-turreted churches. The Jesuits and their missions arrived here from Canada in the 1600s and so everything is Saint this and Pere that.

Marin turned eight last week and she is into butterflies and from up here I can see her net and I can also see Lisa watching her and when she glances up at the house I step away from the window. Why? I don't think about it, I just step away. Marin is wearing the bizarre yellow dress Lisa's mom gave her for her birthday and this afternoon, maybe sooner, we will take a picture of Marin in it to send to her grandmother and then she won't have to wear the dress anymore. Marin is still chasing butterflies with her net but is it just me, or does it look like she's only half-heartedly trying to catch one? There's something *off* about the way she holds the net and I wonder what that says about her desire to catch butterflies, which seems more like playacting desire than genuine desire.

Nonetheless I'm glad we're here, even though I don't like the house.

Or the lake.

Or the village.

Then why am I glad we're here? I don't know. Maybe because Lisa can unwind and even put in some work on her new play. And because I won't be in contact with any of my clients, there will be less distraction and I'll be able to be there for Lisa to bounce dialogue off if she wants to, and who knows, this might be a new chapter for us, a chance for me to really show her that I care about her work. Maybe she will write in the turret, impaired by dampness, and then I will be the one in the garden with the hair standing up on my neck from the feeling of someone watching me.

I hear something outside, like a sharp laugh, but when I look out the window there's no one. Lisa and Marin are no longer in the garden. I hear it again and follow the sound to the greenhouse next to the garden, where I see Lisa holding Marin up by the waist so she can peer into one of the glass panes. The greenhouse looks smaller, less threatening than in years past, but who is to say? Lisa has never liked the greenhouse so maybe that's why she holds Marin up to peer inside rather than just opening the glass door to walk in. Why doesn't Lisa like the greenhouse? Maybe it has something to do with her redacted childhood, visiting this place. (And by redacted I mean all the things she won't tell me.) Or maybe it's a story I told her, early in our marriage, about a client's request that I do his reiteration here.

I must have been deep in a daydream because here is Marin all of a sudden, having tromped up the stairs.

Daddy!

Each time she exclaims that, I'm terrified it will be the last. I was never sentimental until Marin.

Daddy, the greenhouse!

Did Mommy let you look inside?

We *went* inside!

Marin jumps into my arms, squeezes my neck, and then right away wriggles to be let down. I can hear Lisa at the bottom of the stairs and then her voice carrying up: Come on, Marin, she says, let's change you out of that ugly dress.

2.

At dinner that night in the kitchen, with the windows open after putting Marin to bed, I surprise Lisa with a line from one of her plays, weaving it into our conversation. She's dyed her hair blond and it's teased, if that's the right word. It's wavy. For a few flickering seconds she looks like Barbara Crampton from *Chopping Mall*, a movie we were obsessed with on VHS, but I can't hold the image. The movie came out in 1986 (maybe this was around the time Lisa's aunt got hold of that Apple Lisa 2 computer?), although I'm sure we didn't see it until a few years later and the part we loved the most was the scene with the cigarette-vending machine in the s(c)hopping mall. Lisa and I had never been to or heard of a mall that had cigarette-vending machines and we figured that maybe they had them in malls out in unimaginable California, where we assumed *Chopping Mall* had been filmed. Or did they just put it there for the movie so that shirtless Mike would have an excuse to die? And why was Mike shirtless?

Mike was shirtless because (a) he is a hunk and (b) if you are going to slit someone's throat—especially if you're an awkward, clumsy "protector robot"—it's probably going to be easier and more effective blood-wise if the victim is not wearing any clothes on the top part. The robot—they go from "protector" robots designed for mall security to "killbots" after an electrical storm screws up their circuitry—asks for Mike's ID, then it shoots him with a tranquilizer dart, and then it cuts his throat. But it was the greasy cigarette machine we really liked, or the idea of the cigarette machine in a mall.

At dinner that night, I don't remember why, we had drunk almost three bottles of wine that tasted honeyed in a way that suggested tampering. It was one of those muggy summer nights, with everything moving so slow, like time is moving in slo-mo like when you put a 45 on the turntable but the speed is still set at 33⅓ and it sounds like they're playing in molasses. Even the fireflies seem to hold their yellow flashes for longer.

Are you drunk enough to say I love you? I lean over and whisper to Lisa, but when she doesn't react I think maybe I've misquoted her or else quoted from someone else's play.

Are *you*? she says, pouring me another glass.

Doesn't Lisa recognize the line? She wrote it, after all! Or does she recognize it and just pretends not to? But why would she do that? She tousles her hair like she wants to keep the waviness going and tells me that Marin caught a butterfly and when she tried to shake it loose from her net a wing broke and Marin didn't know what to do or how to react. She just stood there, Lisa said, staring at the butterfly flopping in the net, half of what it had been before she caught it.

Maybe it was just a moth, I say. Tell Marin tomorrow it was just a moth.

Just a moth? Jesus, David, Lisa says. She calls me David. Unusual. I'd like to trace the advent of the new Lisa to this moment but that would be a false tracing. Then she says something about Nabokov but I don't get the reference until later, after it's too late. I want to call her Barbara but that will just bring up *Chopping Mall* and I don't want to talk about *Chopping Mall* tonight.

I don't care much for the kitchen, decorated as it is in her dead aunt's idea of northern-Michigan Finnish ruralis. There are battered, scalded-looking copper pans hanging from a rack above the oven. A small-scale replica of a wooden canoe. An old fish-filleting knife in its leather sheath. A dozen or so amateurish clay pots line the shelves beneath the cupboards, and in the middle of the space sits a warped, stained butcher block. Some fat candles look to have been purposely melted just to give them the feeling of having been melted. (You know, that soft feeling you get upon seeing a melted candle.) There is an alarming saltshaker shaped like a cat with wild, bloodshot eyes. You can't help but think that maybe a terrible act of violence or two occurred here once.

I think of asking Lisa if this is how the kitchen was when she visited as a kid but we have entered a phase of marriage where such questions can go screwy somehow. It's a roll of the dice: either she will just answer the question or she will answer it with a volley that I'll have to return, and I never return them well.

I'm not the playwright, after all, *Barbara*.

3.

The next two days are really good, except for the incident.

Lisa makes progress on her (bloodless) play and Marin and I spend a lot of time down at the lake and even go into the village. There is an ice-cream shop there that we frequent, a place decorated in red, white, and blue, with booths built to look like carnival-ride seats. We rent bikes (she just learned to ride without training wheels) and leave them on the sidewalk unchained because that's the kind of safe place this is.

Something strange happens in the ice-cream shop, though. The shop, as are most businesses in the town, is typically staffed by underweight college students earning some summer cash, and last year Marin and one of these worker-students even struck up a short-lived pen-pal friendship. But this year it's the complete opposite: there is only one worker, an enormous man who looks like an ogre. My great grandmother would have called him Eoten. His oversized forehead, heavy eyelids, and dirty face (smudged with coal dust was my first thought) stay focused on the scoops as he serves the ice cream with his large, hairy hands. He seems completely out of place there, as if teleported in from some other time, dragged across the eras from Porvoo, Finland. Even his clothes seem odd, almost like a costume but tattered and worn in a way that seems authentic, especially his leather suspenders, which barely hold his pants up beneath his enormous belly.

In another setting I can picture him in one of the Jesuit black robes, something so dark it absorbs light.

In another setting I can picture him shoving an infidel's face into a cauldron of hot oil.

Daddy, look! Marin says before suddenly remembering her manners. I don't need to tell her that it's not polite to stare. In fact, I don't tell her because her hearing loss has gotten to the point where the rudimentary, pastiche sign language we are slowly developing is more effective than words. I touch her shoulder gently and give her the no-no hand sign. As we pay, the ice-cream man looks into my eyes and my loathing turns to sympathy and then quickly back to loathing and something worse and while Marin takes her cone over to one of the booths I ask him if this is the first summer he's worked here.

I've always worked here, he says, rather dramatically. It catches me off guard. I can't help but noticing how asymmetrical and waxy his face is, splattered with red and black moles like some unfinished Pollock painting, with one eye a good half-inch lower than the other. It's also slightly pointed in the wrong direction. Do they still call them wandering eyes?

Then he says, sort of s(c)hopping-mall like, my name's Paul. Yours?

I introduce myself, and, since there's no one else in the shop but us three, ask him if there is a library in town, which is something I should know after years of coming here, although in my defense we bring our own books to read, as I'm sure many people do on vacation.

He gets distracted when a customer—an old, hunched-over woman wearing a headscarf and with a little white dog in a wicker basket—comes into the shop. She coughs as if to signal something secret. After she leaves, I ask him again, Well, is there?

Is there what?

A library, I say.

A library, he says back, his brow furrowing. It's as if he has never heard the word before. Does he somehow know about Marin's hearing condition and is that why he draws out the word?

Lie-brair-ee, he says.

Something happens behind his eyes, like a whirring, and then he says, the library, yes, three streets over, on Hilldale.

He motions in that direction with his elbow, grotesquely swollen and ripe.

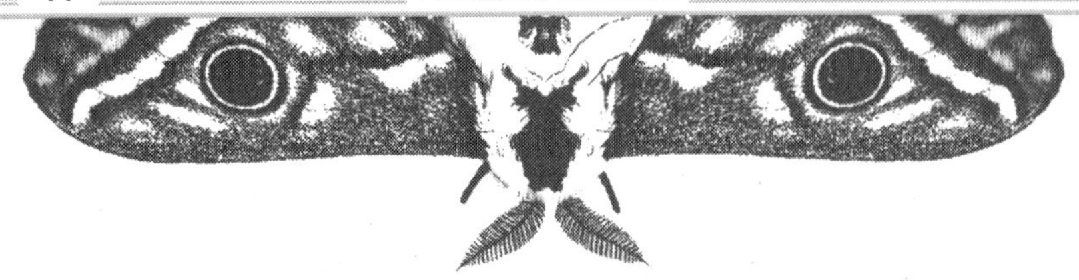

4.

While Marin is on the floor in the library's children's section (which, as expected, smells like crayons and construction paper), I catch a movement, a flutter, from the corner of my eye. It's a moth, on my shoulder, small and rust-colored and freckled like an autumn leaf or a fragment of an autumn leaf except velvety.

Suddenly, Marin turns and looks at me, and then at the moth, her body tensing. Sometimes when she gets like this, her freckles brighten. It's not blushing, exactly, because it's only her freckles that glow. She sets down *The Very Hungry Caterpillar* (with care—she loves this book) and stands up from the floor, her eyes never leaving the moth. Her hair is macraméd in pigtails and she wears fingernail polish for the first time. Yesterday, Lisa and Marin pretended they were at a spa and Lisa painted her nails the color of tangerines. For a few moments Marin stands there awkwardly with her arms to her sides like one of those creepy kids (or were they short adults in kids' outfits?) from that Cronenberg film *The Brood*. (Lisa and I are split on this one. It's a favorite of mine, but she hates it and still brings it up that I made her watch it.) But then Marin comes over and gently cups the little moth between her hands and I stand up and walk with her to the library entrance, opening the door for her to let the moth go.

There is a librarian with soft, kind eyes behind the checkout desk, her silver hair long and straight. She wears funky pink glasses. She must be in her '60s or '70s and yet you can just tell she feels herself to look so much younger.

I don't trust her or her generation of murderers.

She watches as Marin walks carefully, like she's on a balance beam, with the moth, and there is a moment—a perfect moment—as I push open the door for Marin and the moth, when the librarian seems about to come over to help, but then decides to let Marin save the moth on her own. I am stunned by the sound the door makes as I open it, *swish*, like I've activated a portal to some alien world.

If only.

If only it could be that Marin and I walked out of this library and into an alien landscape with towering cactus-like trees and a vast veldt and a yellow sky with three enormous moons on the horizon. I can imagine there is something hovering in the sky in the distance, a floating steel ship tethered to the ground with heavy black chains. Buildings covered in thick green moss, and there is a crimson glow behind each of the windows, and Marin, too, can hear every sound, even that of the tree buds opening. Even the chirping of crickets one hundred miles away in some forgotten meadow. If only it could be like that. If only it could be like that forever.

Marin is quiet in the car on the way back to the cottage, except to say, Don't tell Mom.

I want to ask, *Don't tell mom what?* because it was just a moth and it wasn't hurt.

But it seems Marin is piecing it out in her head, too, and if I ask her why not tell Mom she might not know the answer. Since her hearing loss began last year, she seems to live in her head more and more. Is this just developmental, typical for a seven-year-old (or is she eight?), or is it related to her condition? They call it sensorineural hearing loss, having to do with a nerve in her inner ears, supposedly. It's apparently rare to have it in both ears, but they say she does. The strange thing is, she doesn't seem to notice it, maybe because it's been so gradual it feels normal to her.

On our way back to the house we get lost (the sun doesn't seem right and I get confused) and end up on a narrow road in the forest. At one point the overstory is so thick and heavy I need to turn on the headlights. One of the massive roadside trees—an oak from the elbowing bends of its branches—is carved with a large awkward heart with initials inside that are hard to make out but appear to be K+M.

I remember this only because just below the heart is a painted red X. Not spray-painted but as if brushed on. I don't know why this gives me a scare. It reminds me of something I can't quite bring into focus, an image that keeps skirting off into the far edge of peripheral vision. If it peeks too close I blot it out. Marin points at the red X in a swish of tangerine and wants to stop but I keep going. I try to change the subject, reminding her of the ice cream from earlier but she persists and then pouts. I know it won't last long and so I take advantage of the silence and absorb the landscape of this unfamiliar part of the country.

I'm not supposed to be thinking about any of my clients or their reiterations, especially client J, and yet here I am thinking about them, client M in particular, whom I only met once. For all I know, client M doesn't represent just himself but rather a group of people, a conglomerate, or even a corporation, or an entity of some sort, or maybe even a government. After M, I decided never to meet my clients face to face, that it would be easier if I didn't have a sense of who they were in the physical sense. I could look them up of course, but what does a picture say, really, especially since it could be as fake as the one I used for myself online?

Marin is still sulking in the back seat.

Poutmouth, I say, and that gets her, like it always does. In the rearview mirror I see her smile, and then she gives me a raspberry. We are out of the heavy damnous woods now and I'm still lost. I don't have my phone with me. I keep driving and the sun comes out from behind the clouds and soon we are in a completely different landscape, open low meadows and no houses or buildings except for a red barn (which I imagine being held down with huge underground chains that lead directly to Hell) in the distance.

Daddy, Old MacDonald! Marin shrieks.

She has been listening to that song on the toy record player she got for Christmas. When she sings it, sometimes she says *with a wolf wolf here and a wolf wolf there* instead of *woof woof*. I think she knows it's a dog but she wants it to be a wolf and at first I thought she had heard it wrong and wanted to correct her but Lisa, rightly so, said to just let her say it that way, what does it matter? Why correct her all the time, reminding her of what's happening inside her ears? Just let her be, David, she tells me, just let her be.

5.

Back at the cottage, it's very quiet. Lisa is upstairs, in the bedroom or the underproportioned turret, probably working on her new play. This is one of the last happy days I remember, before the catastrophe of the Lisa 2 computer and the genre switch to what Lisa would come to call *notional horror*, an obscure term that I tried to tell her would never catch on. The kitchen window is open and a warm, sweet breeze ruffles the pink paper napkins on the table. It was Marin's birthday yesterday, thus the pink napkins, the pink candles, the pink stuffed unicorn, all clashing with the tangerine nails. I listen for sounds of Lisa while Marin climbs the wooden stool to get a glass from the cupboard. I, in turn, climb the stairs to Lisa, as if . . . *As if what?* As if there's an intruder in the house who has done something terrible to her with his metallic, talon-like fingernails and so I need to be very quiet, very careful not to alert this psycho fuck to my presence on the stairs. As usual, there's no intruder, but there is something surprising. Instead of sitting at the wooden desk that faces the window looking out onto the lake, Lisa is on the bed, on her back, sleeping, her arms spread out, her neck vulnerable. An image flashes into my head from *At Land,* that Maya Deren film we were so obsessed with early in our marriage. Maya Deren on the beach, alive and dead at the same time.

Like Deren, Lisa looks peaceful and open and I imagine that if I sat down on the bed it might go something like this, as if Lisa had written it under the influence of Lisa 2 . . .

DAVID: I wondered what was going on up here
LISA: And I wondered when you'd come up to find out. Tell me about the moth.
DAVID: How do you know about that? Was Marin up here? I didn't see her come up.
LISA: Because she didn't.
DAVID: Then how do you know about the moth?
LISA: You wouldn't believe me if I told you.
DAVID: Try me.
LISA: I was dreaming about it. Just now. A little brown thing, furry. On Marin's shoulder. You cup it in your hands and take it outside and let it go.

DAVID: How do you know all that?

LISA: I don't know how I know. I think it's this melting room. There's something about this room. Put your hands around my throat and squeeze and all your problems will be solved.

. . . except that Lisa's plays are not anything like this. There's nothing naturalistic or frightening about them. That's the whole point of her project, and by *project* I mean all her writing, all her plays up until she began using the Lisa 2 computer to compose them, or should I say until the computer started using Lisa to compose them? But I'm getting ahead of myself, because in order for the computer debacle to make sense I first have to make clear that Lisa would never write anything as straightforward as the moth dream, and I doubt she would even use the plain-speaking word *moth* to describe the moth and she would definitely not write about choking someone to death.

But she *would* describe the upstairs bedroom that way, *this melting room*.

That's a phrase she'd use. I don't wake her, though I do steal a glance at the pages on her desk. She writes the first draft in longhand and I see that she has placed little pieces of black electrical tape over the characters' names. Which is weird. Why would she bother to tape over them rather than simply cross them out? In fact, why even cross them out at all? For a moment I fear that if I turn to look at Lisa sleeping on the bed I'll see black X's over *her* eyes, like in an old cartoon, or even worse: if I look over at her it will be *me* who has the X's over *his* eyes and that I'll be standing here, Nosferatu-pale, rigid, half-dead.

A half-dead man standing.

A half-dead man dreaming.

Blood draining down from his eyes onto his face and then, when the drops hit the floor, blossoming into flowers whose blooms look like the crushed bodies of moths. But why do I think this? Where in the world has this thought come from?

I hear a thump, and then another, and then the sound of Marin running up the stairs and then there she is behind me, barefoot.

Why is Mommy sleeping?

Not sleeping, Lisa says, sitting up. Just resting my eyes.

Marin hops onto the bed and says, Trap me!

Their old game where Lisa traps her with her legs and Marin squeals and wriggles as she tries to get out.

(There will also be a last time for this game and I can't bear to think of it because you never know when it's going to be the last time and I almost cry at the joy and sadness of seeing Lisa and Marin playing like this.)

The kitchen phone rings. The house still has one of those, an old rotary one. That sickening, wobbly ring. It gives me a chance to exit (*stage left*, Lisa might say), but of course by the time I arrive the phone has stopped ringing. After a moment it begins again. I answer but there's no response. Stupidly, like in the movies, I say (in a voice not unlike that of the Suzie character in *Chopping Mall*), Who's there, who is this? There's no answer, only the low hiss of black static. I hold the receiver away from my ear as if that will change anything. Is this a protector? I ask. Upstairs I hear Lisa and Marin still playing and laughing on the bed. Then I have a chilling thought: it's client M who's on the other end of the line. I have to admit it's not the first time the thought has crossed my mind. On the drive up here, for instance, that shiny black car with the tinted windshields following us. I even pulled into a gas station just to see what would happen and sure enough so did the car, idling there behind me. But then at the next stop sign—the first one before the village, actually—the car turned right while we kept going straight onto the road that runs around the lake.

But why would M follow me, especially in a black car with tinted windows? Right out of some cheap movie. Maybe it's something Lisa could use for one of her plays, not that she writes thrillers or anything even close, although there is something recently scary, something icy, about her work. I press the receiver tight against my ear and for some reason think of Lisa's aunt Elle, dead now, doing the same thing on this same phone, how many times? It's got to be from the '70s, this phone, a shade of offensive plastic brown they don't make anymore. How many ears had pressed against it, and now mine? I think I detect something beneath the static, a whisper, a whisper behind the whisper, and then another whisper behind that, and behind all those layers a dead sound.

Something is beginning to happen, and maybe it's time to bring it to a head.

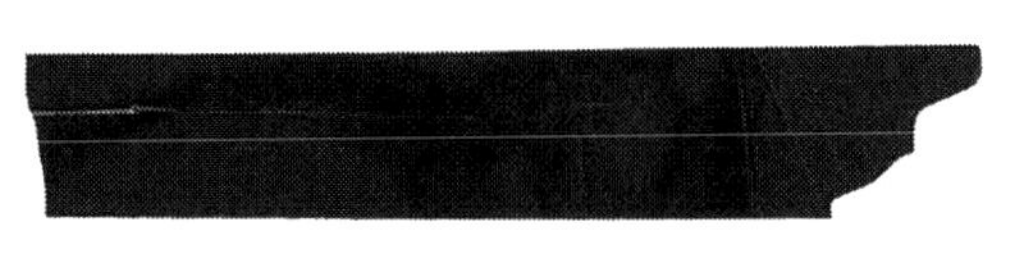

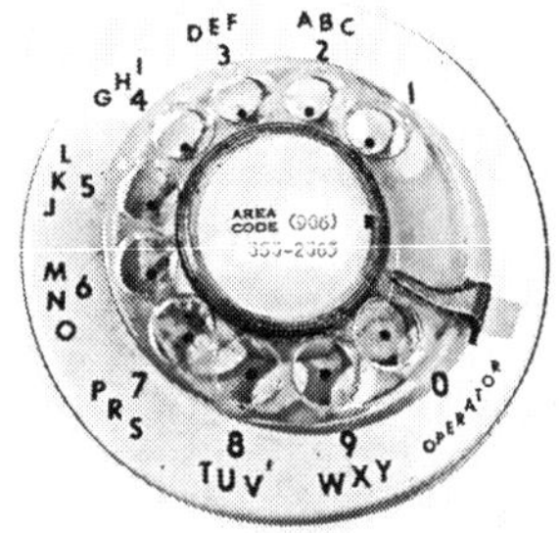

6.

One of the fascinations of aunt Elle's cottage is that it's like a time capsule, with updates. There is the kitchen phone, of course, and the fashionable-again avocado-green stove, and the unsteady lamps with their stiff brown cords. The ruby glass in the cupboard. The faded pink shag carpeting in the bathroom, which extends even to the toilet seat. The perfume bottles with their yellowed labels, still half empty, in the upstairs bedroom. The glass gloom chasers stuck to the front bay window by small plastic suction cups that don't seem to have been moved since the '70s.

The gold butterfly.

The yellow daisy flower.

The girl with the red demon face.

And in the storage closet beneath the stairs are several old typewriters and early computers, including the rotten Apple Lisa 2, a dot-matrix printer, plus several boxes of floppy disks. Aunt Elle had supposedly been an accountant for SafeArms, the local insurance company up here which insured Anthony "Tony Jack" Giacalone (who, they say, disappeared Hoffa), and I say *supposedly* because Lisa's family is known for tall tales when it comes to relatives, especially the further back you go, e.g., "we're related to Annie Oakley" or "was the third cousin of Ulysses S. Grant" or "played a small but important part at the Jamestown colony" or "ran maintenance for the Pittsburgh Pirates' scoreboard in the '60s."

It's a shiny morning and in the kitchen sunlight the phone no longer looks sinister.

I'm making French toast for Marin and we have got our little routine. I crack two eggs (cage-free, though, as Lisa reminds me, even that's problematic) in the glass bowl, splash in some oat milk and whisk it up. Marin drops the bread in, lets it soak for a second, and then flips it over with tongs to get the other side. Then she takes it out and places it on the hot skillet already sputtering with plant butter. It's a big deal for her to do this right and I have to be careful not to say *good job!* She pours the orange juice, puts the syrup on the table, and even asks me to do my Mrs. Butterworth's impersonation, which I always fear will be the last time.

A last time for calling me Daddy, a last time for letting me swoop her up in my arms, a last time for reading her a bedtime story, a last time for Mrs. B.

Lisa joins us, coming up from behind to give me a hug. In the window reflection I see she has braided her Barbara Crampton hair. There is something about the angle of the sun on the lake out the window and the long, early-morning pine-tree shadows cast across it that seems aching and impossible, like nothing that could occur naturally in nature.

Why does this flash of beauty shock me?

Have I lost my ability to just see things in the world as they are?

Why should I be surprised that the natural world could offer up something so spectacular, not so dependent on human interference? Maybe I'll mention this to Lisa as a thought for a future play, something that harkens back to her early work, her *Walden* cycle. Actually, her source was Thoreau's lesser-known work *Cape Cod*, published a decade after *Walden*, but audiences assumed *Walden* was the inspiration (and with a title like *Walled-In*, who could blame them?), and in fact, the marketing materials for the play even featured a rendering of a pond.

For her birthday that year, just as she was completing the final draft, I bought her an old copy of *Cape Cod*, not the first edition, from 1865, but an 1893 reprint. Although I don't think she ever used it, I read it—even the boring parts that just described plants and rocks with no commentary, no distinguishable authorial voice—and one part has always stuck with me, where Thoreau quotes the eighteenth-century naturalist David Crantz, who in turn quotes someone named Dalagen:

> Crantz, in his account of Greenland, quotes Dalagen's relation of the ways and usages of the Greenlanders, and says, "Whoever finds drift-wood, or the spoils of a shipwreck on the strand, enjoys it as his own, though he does not live there. But he must haul it ashore and lay a stone upon it, as a token that someone has taken possession of it, and this stone is the deed of security, for no other Greenlander will offer to meddle with it afterwards."

I always loved this image of the rock on the driftwood and when I found just such a thing down at the beach that summer I had to remind myself that it was me who put the stone on top of it.

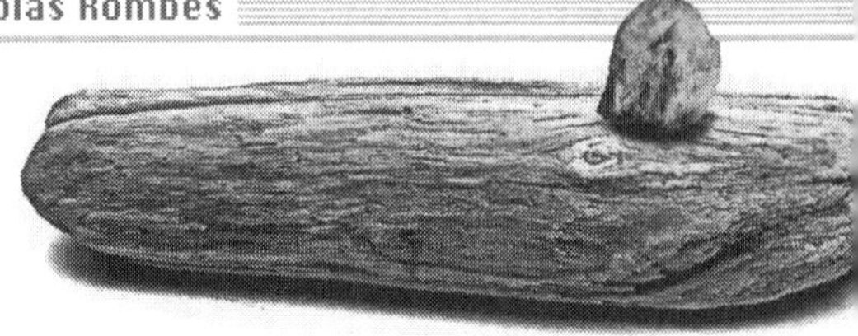

7.

There's something about this room. I'm back in the house, in the kitchen, and that line from the play I imagine Lisa is writing drifts back into my mind. I can hear her movements upstairs, at her writing desk, and I know things are going well because she doesn't say anything when she hears me come in. This is when I notice the door in the kitchen. Not the door leading out back, but an interior one, on the wall opposite the phone. We spend only a few weeks here each summer, and some summers not at all, so it's possible the door has always been there and I've just now noticed. It's behind a low, beat-up sideboard where we keep stuff we don't use much: a box of Fourth of July napkins and paper plates and plastic tablecloths, a rusted pocket knife, that sort of thing. So it's not like the whole door's visible, which makes me feel better. Easy to have missed.

And yet.

I make a note to check it out later, or maybe I will now, but then I hear a thump from up in Marin's room and I go to the bottom of the stairs to listen.

and you sit there . . .

no, not there, there . . .

She's probably playing tea with the old dishes we found in the basement yesterday. I pause, hand on the banister, and let it all soak in: the quiet of the house, my wife and daughter lost in their imaginary worlds, the peace that comes from knowing that right now nothing bad can happen, that reality is unfolding in just the way I want it to, almost scripted, with no surprises, no ambushes. I close my eyes. The ultimate reiteration.

no, Jayson, I said not there . . .

I don't think I've heard Marin correctly; I can't have. Did she say *Jayson*? Before it sinks in, Lisa comes down the stairs, pages in hand.

Can I borrow you for a sec?

Of course, I say. She is so geeky right now, in this light, on the stairs, her Crampton hair liberated from its braids, her face a little flushed, a vibe bordering on the alarming, which is the only way I can describe it when she's in the creative groove and the ideas and words are flowing. Before she even reaches me at the bottom of the stairs she hands me a page.

You're Paul, she says, and I'm Julia.

Okay, I say.

I follow her into the kitchen, trailing in the wake of her enthusiasm.

Paul's the guy's name from the shop, I say.

The shop?

The ice-cream shop Marin and I went to, the worker dude's name is Paul.

Okay, Paul, she says, grinning, read your lines.

I love this part of the process and know that by the time she asks me to do this she has already decided it's a good scene and now she wants to hear it to make little adjustments.

JULIA: **Come on, you can be honest, man!**
PAUL: ***Man*? Since when do you call me that?**
JULIA: **Isn't that what it was all about last night? You trying to be a *man*?**
PAUL: **Trying? Do you think . . .**

Lisa interrupts. She is worried about the *that what* wording in Julia's second line. She changes it and we do it again.

JULIA: Come on, you can be honest man!
PAUL: Man? Since when do you call me that?
JULIA: Last night—weren't you trying to be a man?
PAUL: Trying? Do you think I have to try?
JULIA: Braces, Paul, really? How old was she, eighteen?
PAUL: Twenty-year-olds wear braces too. It's a thing now.
JULIA: It's a thing, or it's a thing now in porn?

It's good, I said. It's groovy.

Groovy?

You know what I mean. It moves, it's lean.

Do you think it's a little too *Who's Afraid of Virginia Woolf*-y?

No, but I'm not sure you need to italicize the word man.

The audience won't know it's italicized, she says.

But the actor will, I say.

I'm only doing this because if I just tell her I love it she won't believe me. I have to give her some feedback or else my opinion is worthless. I've learned with Lisa that I have to *earn* the praise I give her by also offering some sort of critique.

You're right, she says, I'll take the quotes off.

Good job, *man*, I say.

Lisa laughs and goes back upstairs.

8.

The first package arrives the next day, or within a few days at least. A brown envelope that when I pick it up off the porch I immediately think there will be a hat inside, a wool hat, a black wool hat, a black wool hat for a man, a black wool hat for me. Of course, it's something far more sinister than a black wool hat for a man (as if a black wool hat could be sinister to begin with), but at the moment, at least, like Schrödinger's cat, it is simultaneously a black wool hat and not a black wool hat.

For some reason, I think back to that movie where the woman finds a package outside her door with a VHS tape inside that, when she plays it, shows her filmed as if from across the street, retrieving that very package from outside her door.

Impossible!

Her husband's a jazz saxophonist, I think, and there's a weird scene where he calls her from the jazz club and he's all bathed in red light. I can't remember the name of the movie or any of the actors but I remember watching it with Lisa and she just laughed.

What a silly movie, she had said.

Or maybe, What an absurd movie.

It's a film by David Lynch, I'm remembering now. But Lisa did end up lifting at least one line of dialogue from the film. The powerful, menacing guy in the film is being tailgated on a winding mountain road and it really pisses him off. He stops suddenly, gets out of his car, goes over to the poor tailgater and pulls him out of *his* car, throws him to the ground, takes out his gun and screams at him, I want you to get a fuckin' drivers' manual, and I want you to study that motherfucker! It's a scary scene but it's also really funny, or at least it was before road rage became a thing.

What's in the package isn't anything like a black wool hat at all but rather something in Bubble Wrap. At first I think it's a dead thing, like a taxidermied bird, because it's brown and feathery. But it turns out not to be feathers at all but something like a soft brown moss lightly covering what appears to be a piece of tree bark, about the size of, well, a black hat. And carved roughly into that piece of bark are these printed letters: K + M with an X beneath, like this:

K + M
X

Where have I seen this before? The forest, of course, that fucking time I got lost driving back from the library with Marin. There are no markings on the package; it hasn't been mailed but rather left there and I go to the door and look out. I wonder if it's been taken from the tree itself. The easiest way to find out is to go back into town, maybe with Marin again, and try to retrace the route home that got us lost in the forest. Then, as if on cue, Marin bounds into the room.

Daddy, what? she asks, as if I had called out to her.

9.

I decided today I hate Julia, Lisa says.

We have just put Marin to bed and are downstairs in the kitchen. I'm doing the dishes and Lisa's standing at the never-bloodied butchers block with a glass of water. I can't help but think they should have had a scene like this in *Chopping Mall*. What a wasted opportunity! The hardware store was so obvious, but what about the kitchen store, with its carving knives and meat grinders and garbage disposals and anticipatory butcher blocks? Poor Barbara Crampton wouldn't have stood a chance with a blender.

You mean your friend Julia, or Julia in the play? I ask.

The one in the play, she says. I can't make her real.

Maybe that's because there's already a real one. Just change her name.

I'm joking, but only sort of. In her plays, Lisa tends to use the names of people she knows, which means I can never fall completely under their spell because I'm always thinking of the people she has named characters after, even though most of the time these characters bear no resemblance. Julia, for instance, Lisa's oldest friend, from high school. What some people might call a free spirit, a post-hippie hippie (and wide-hipped), never owned a home, rarely wore shoes, never lived in the same town for more than a few years. The complete opposite, lifestyle-wise, from the Julia in Lisa's play, which has a working title now: *Doubting Thomasina*.

Lisa and I have evolved into this obscure mid-marriage thing where we don't talk about each other to each other. Maybe it started around the time of Marin's arrival. All we talked about was Marin (a toddler absorbs all information; nothing can escape), and then when Lisa started writing again all we talked about was her plays, and then when I started doing my reiterations again (I called them removals or copies back then) all we talked about was those.

There were exceptions: Lisa's sister's suicide took up some talking.

So did the terrorist poisoning of all those kids who drank from the drinking fountains in the Los Angeles public schools. Actually, that was around the time we decided to switch the name from copies to reiterations. I advertised what I did, of course, but Lisa and I were in agreement that what I practiced (insofar as she knew what it was I did) had to have a better name, just like what she did had a name. After a while, copies somehow seemed too sinister, and so I destroyed all my business cards (Lisa insisted I have them for the legitimacy they conferred) and had new ones printed: Reiterative Specialist.

Lisa glances over at the stairs.

I'm either going to make her real tomorrow or finish her off, she says. I assume she's talking about Julia from the play. She turns to go upstairs and flicks off the kitchen light, leaving me in the dark.

Hey! I say.

She laughs and turns it back on. It's an old routine of hers that began when we were dating, an ingrained habit from her childhood, where she was raised to turn off the lights in rooms when she left, even if it was just to go into another room for a few seconds. But now she does it as a joke, sort of. I think she thinks it's a gag that Mel Brooks would approve. I notice the door beneath the stairs is cracked open and I when I go to shut it I see it there, right where it should be, the Apple Lisa, unused, I imagine, for so long. I pull the door shut and press my palm against it, knowing that, for tonight at least, everything is in its proper place.

10.

It's morning and I'm alone in the house. It's already warm, and Lisa and Marin must be down at the lake. There are pages of Lisa's play on the kitchen table, which, oddly, is covered with a bright new red-checked tablecloth that I have never seen before, and for a moment I feel as if nothing is secure: not this kitchen, not this cottage, not those trees outside, not me. I accept this feeling, maybe because it comes only once in a long while, a sense of floating just outside yourself, not separated but hinged or connected by a few threads or fibers, like double vision where both images overlap just a bit, the same but different, especially in the overlapping space. If only I could get that parallel self to snap the threads and break free and go on without me.

I pick up the pages and see right away that something is wrong. It's Lisa's words, but not the same Lisa.

PAUL: No, it's a *thing* thing, not just a porn thing.

JULIA: A *thing* thing? That's absurd.
PAUL: You're absurd.

Deep growl from offstage. The stage lights flicker, dim, go off, and come back on.

JULIA: I think it's here for you.
PAUL: Why me? I'm not the one who pissed it off.
JULIA: Eighteen.
PAUL: She wasn't eighteen.
JULIA: You don't do eighteen and not piss something off. It will come for you directly.
PAUL: If it does come for me, you won't be able to see it.
JULIA: I'll hear it.
PAUL: No pleasure but in meanness.
JULIA: You can't even quote it correctly. You're no Flannery.
PAUL: Anyways, something can't come if there's nothing there to come.
JULIA: So you're calling it *something* now. Not a *thing*.
PAUL: What do you want me to call it?
JULIA: What growls and has horns?

None of it makes sense, at least not in a Julia way. For one thing, the horror part, because if there's a type or genre that Lisa doesn't connect with, it's horror, and I cannot recall one moment in any of her plays that sounds anything like this. And why are these toxic pages even here, sitting out on the kitchen table, as if Lisa has ever left her work just lying around like this? For a moment I have the absurd thought that these are not even her pages, that some *other* Lisa has left them here.

I said *for a moment* but it's not just for a moment. The thought sticks and I'm just standing there, in the morning sun, dumbstruck by the idea that there's *another Lisa*, or another version of Lisa that has somehow replaced the one I know. The next question is, when did this happen? And did it happen all at once or gradually, over time? And does Marin know? Can she sense it too?

Here they come, up from the lake. First, the sound of their laughter carried on the breeze, then I see them between the pine trees, Marin with the sunflower-yellow beach towel draped over her neck and hanging down to her ankles, her wet black hair stuck to her neck in strands. As they pass by the firepit, with a flick of her wrist Lisa tosses something into it and I catch this only because of the little puff of ash that plumes up. Why would she do that?

I go out onto the back deck.

Daddy, the fish, Marin says, jumping into my arms.

Did you catch it?

No, Lisa says. Death caught it.

But Marin isn't smiling. It smelled bad, she says.

We buried it in the sand, didn't we Marin?

Marin doesn't hear her, so Lisa says it again, louder, almost in a scolding way if you didn't know anything about Marin's hearing condition.

We buried it in the sand, didn't we, Marin?

Marin still doesn't hear so Lisa says it again, almost screaming: We buried it in the sand, didn't we Marin?

Marin pushes her face into my shoulder and says, *Mommy* buried it.

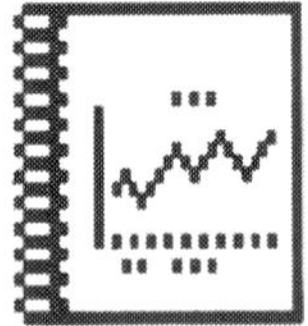

11.

I wait until it's dark, and Lisa is taking a bath, to go fetch whatever it is she chucked into the fire pit. We have had so many campfires out here, roasting marshmallows and all the rest, but of course I'm always thinking of what lies beneath. Beneath the campfire, I imagine its embers warming to some deeper eternal furnace and I think if only I could crawl in there, underneath the warm ashes, and just curl up and listen, I could hear it, the sounds of Hell, which I imagine are like one long, droning note, forever unchanging. That's what Hell is like: a place where nothing changes and yet where time still moves.

With a flashlight and a stick, I poke around in the ashes until I find it, a purple plastic lighter, a BIC and as I'm wiping it clean I feel the etching before I see it.

Kimmy X.

Neatly etched into the side, maybe with a pin. *Kimmy X.* The owner's name? Did Lisa find this on the beach and just toss it here rather than in the garbage? For God's sake, why would she do such a thing? I shake it and there is still a little fluid, and then I flick it on, my thumb over that rough little wheel, and just as the flame pops up, a light comes on in the house, from our bedroom. Has Lisa seen me, and if so, so what? I'm not the one who ditched the lighter in the firepit, and yet it somehow feels suspicious, me being out here in the dark, scamping around rather than just asking her what it was she tossed. A wind moves through the pines and there is a call from a distant night bird (enormous, I imagine) that must nest down by the lake. Not so much a call as a yip or a howl, like a coyote. The light in the bedroom window goes out and when I'm back inside I drop the lighter into the kitchen junk drawer and pour myself a glass of milk. Maybe she'll see it and say something like Oh the lighter, yeah, I found it down by the dead fish and tossed it into the ashes because it stunk.

The pages from the table are missing. She must have taken them back upstairs to work on them tomorrow and I'm just as glad they're gone. So what if Lisa is evolving into a new, different sort of writer? Just because her writing has changed doesn't mean *she's* changed, right? She is an artist after all, a creator, a maker, and when I think about the writers she admires it's the ones who don't create the same sort of world every time, the ones who risk something new, the ones who widen, rather than restrict, the ragged territory of their imaginations. Why should she stick to writing the same play over and over again, and why should it bother me if she does? I'm not that sort of husband. Lisa's creativity and success don't bother me.

Upstairs, on the way to the bedroom, I peek into Lisa's writing room. Why should I be surprised to see the framed black-and-white photo of Zora Neale Hurston on the desk? Lisa wrote her master's thesis on Hurston's work in Haiti, and the photo—taken by Alan Lomax in the mid-'30s—shows Hurston, in Florida, collecting songs from Rochelle French and Gabriel Brown. But even from here, standing in the doorway, I can see there is something wrong with the photo.

I approach closer. In the moonlight I see right away what ails it. There, between the men, is a small, gray, vertical line, just floating. I know this is not part of the photo, or at least it shouldn't be. Does Lisa know it's there? Did she make this alteration? Or does it have something to do with Lisa 2? When I lean in closer I notice something else: it appears as if Hurston herself is gazing at the gray line, like she is holding it there, as it floats, with her eyes.

I'm beginning to understand what's happening.

I crawl into bed with Lisa and try to pretend everything is okay.

12.

The easiest way to talk to Marin alone is to take her back into town, and since she begs to go to the ice-cream shop, that's where we end up. It's one of those brilliant bright days, the sky so clear that it feels like there is no barrier between the earth and the universe. The clouds have moved on, the sky has sharpened, and at the top of the ridge before descending into the village you can see forever. We pull over and climb on top of the car. I hoist Marin onto my shoulders and ask her what she sees.

The sky!

What else? I ask.

The tower, she says. It's upside down.

I can see the bell tower, too, a part of the church, and it's not upside down.

No, it's not, silly, I say.

No response.

No, it's not, silly, I repeat, louder.

Yes it is, and it's *moving*.

Marin's always been this imaginative, and every once in a while it frightens us.

There's someone in my closet, she'd say, and of course that was understandable, natural, even. What child *hasn't* believed there is something in their closet that should not be there, a trespasser with sharp, oversized bronze claws and a face that looked like melted wax.

Marin has tea with her invisible friends all the time, and she tucks her dolls in and sings them good-night songs. But then sometimes she stumped us. The time she saw the white sailboat on the lake that neither of us could see. The morning she said she was sorry about my bad dream and then described it, incorrectly, but with a few details that were pretty close. I guess that's just part of what makes Marin Marin, and the force of her personality and imagination is something we're proud of, as if we have anything to do with it.

But lately she has been a fantasist in a different sort of way, imagining that there is something wrong with me, although maybe *wrong* is too strong a word. And it's not like she will come right out and say, Daddy, what's wrong? Rather, it's a look she gives. Not even that, really. It's harder to explain. It's there in the pauses between her words. The little spaces where a different, clouded sort of meaning grows. It's here that I detect Marin's concern, as if she senses that something is not right with me, or maybe not right with me and her mom. Maybe that's it—it's not about me but about *us*, us as a family.

The ice-cream shop—Three Scoops is the name—is the same as it was the other week, as if we had just stepped out for a moment and come back in. The ominous Paul-person is there, even more malignant in his largeness than before, mythologically large it seems, his hands monstrous as they dig into the ice cream tub with the metal scoop like it's some sort of surgical instrument. His face is dirty, like before, as if powdered in a reddish ash, or dried blood that has become powdered and looks like ash. He wears that old-world leather apron, grotesquely smeared with all the colors of ice cream, as violent as an aborted Francis Bacon canvas.

You two, he says.

Does he recognize us from the last time?

Paul, I say, right?

Right you are.

He fixes me with a stare. There's something going on there behind his dazed, glassy eyes. His hands, his body, his whole being feels like a threat somehow, lumbered in from the rotting, cockroached medieval past and here before me now in the form of this Paul-person.

He turns his face to Marin.

What will it be today? Strawberry?

He says this loudly, clearly, slowly, as if he knows about her hearing condition. It feels to me like he has violated her somehow, and in the split second before she answers I worry that her response—any response to him—will somehow validate that violation, as if in responding she, at the same time, will tacitly agree to his conditions and terms, which are that she is, and always has been and always will be, his.

But she doesn't answer. Instead, she turns to me.

Cherry, I say to Paul, for both of us.

Is it just me, or does a look of defeat cross his face?

Did you find the lie-brair-ee, he asks, handing us our cones.

He asks it like it was just yesterday.

The library on Hilldale, he says, as if there's another one. That's where they keep the deep history, he says, if that's what you're looking for. You have to ask for it at the reference desk, and don't take no for an answer. You may have to ask three times.

While he's been talking, his eyes have been alive, but when he's finished and has handed me my change they go stale again.

The sun is bright outside and Marin and I cross the street and stroll over to the little park to sit on a bench. Each of the benches here is dedicated to someone, and the little brass nameplate on this one reads: *In Memory of Both My Wives, Doris and Sheryl*. There is really no way to ask Marin directly about Lisa. But what if I just came out with it: Have you noticed anything strange about Mommy lately?

I think he's a Libra, she says.

Who, the ice-cream man? Why do you think so?

I can tell.

What about Mommy, do you remember what she is?

Mommy's nothing, and you're a Leo, and I'm a Gemini.

No, that's not right. Mommy's an Aries, I say.

Marin's working on her cone.

She's smart and she's too hot to handle!

Too hot to handle! Where'd you hear that?

Daddy, the cartoon!

Which one?

She doesn't hear me.

Which *one*?

The one Mommy made, with the wolf.

Maybe she's talking about Lisa's doodles, which show up on our wall calendars, shopping lists, and sometimes the pages of her plays.

In her secret book, Marin says.

I almost don't want to respond for fear it will break or shatter whatever might come next. If I act surprised she might stop for fear of betraying Lisa, but if I act like I know about it there is no need for her to reveal any more. I take a gamble.

Which secret book?

You know, she says, the one in the greenhouse.

13.

Mel calls. He never calls. Mel is the perfect client: I never see him. And rarely hear from him. I'm designing a reiteration for him, a fairly intricate one that involves replacing with a harmless phone call a phone call he shouldn't have made six years ago. Although this reiteration just involves voice actors it's still difficult; it turns out it's easier to fool reality with images than with sounds. The human voice is difficult to imitate.

How much am I paying you? Mel asks.

Mel, I say. You never ask that question.

But now that it's been asked, he says.

You're not supposed to.

To what?

To ask. That question.

The phone is hot in my hand. I'm in the kitchen, of course. The old phone with its long yellow cord, like fusilli. I twist it around my finger, an old nervous tic.

Am I the only one? he says.

I feel sorry for him.

I have many clients, I say.

In my father's house are many mansions, he mimics.

Come on, I say, not now.

How much am I paying you? he asks.

In dollars or rupees?

Don't kid with me, he says. There is a hitch in his voice. I've heard what Mel can do to a human body—I've seen pictures, actually—and so I answer.

Two million, I say.

It's the truth: he is paying me a lot of money, and part of the agreement—the *understanding*—is that he not ask me how much he's paying me. This question could void the contract, but the thing with Lisa maybe not being the Lisa I used to know has spooked me and I go along with his little game, hoping he'll let it drop.

And for how many reiterations? he asks.

For just the one.

He knows this, of course. We negotiated it over several months, ironing out all the wrinkles, all the ambiguities. One iteration = two million. On the phone, I let him breathe. This, in my experience, is the best response. Let them breathe, and in their breathing let them think about what it is they're asking, because they already know the answers to their questions. The phone cord is now wrapped around several fingers as well as around my elbow, and I'm caught in a web of excess, ridiculous cord. How I hate this scheming cottage! As Mel breathes and I wait, I hear Marin coming down the stairs for breakfast.

It'll be complete by next week, Mel, just as we agreed, I say finally. You don't need to call again.

I hang up just as Marin throws her arms around my waist.

Pancakes or waffles? I ask. She's wearing her yellow pajamas.

Waffles!

Waffles and what?

Whipped cream! And cherry sauce.

We don't have cherry sauce.

Pause.

We don't have cherry sauce.

Then extra whipped cream!

I just want to spend this morning with Marin because I know someday her world and mine will become separate. She will keep more and more of her thoughts to herself, as it should be. But for now, while her world and mine overlap, circle each other in the same gravitational field, I just want to let it be. So, I take the phone off the hook and set it on the counter. No more interruptions from Mel. Only later—when it's too late—will I learn that the next call, had it come through, wasn't from Mel, but from the person who left the package with the marked tree bark.

14.

The next day Lisa comes back from town with a fresh, short haircut. Goodbye, Barbara Crampton, hello Sigourney Weaver a la *Alien 3*. She wears the most sparkling, vibrant-green eyeshadow I've ever seen her in and it reminds me of her old obsession with Cyndi Lauper. Lisa's hair is cut sharp above the ears, with her little sideburns in a V-shape. I tell her she looks like a Hemingway girl and she grins. I'm making chili in the kitchen, my cutting board covered with neat, palm-sized piles of chopped onions, carrots, and celery. The spices here in the cupboard are Aunt Elle's, little faded red McCormick tin canisters that must be decades old. But the chili powder still smells like chili powder and the cumin like cumin. They'll do. Anyways, if there are rust flakes in the chili powder, how to tell?

Not a Murakami girl? Lisa 2 asks, tugging on her earlobe.

I want to say no, a Lauper girl, but that would just open up old wounds.

Guh-guh-girls just want . . . she says.

She comes up behind me and puts her arms around me and for a moment I can pretend she is the First Version Lisa, as I've come to think of her. First Lisa. Lisa 1.0. I want to ask her about the Hurston photo but I'm afraid of what she might say. From behind she puts her hand atop mine, which is holding the knife to work on the vegetables, and together we chop the carrots. The window above the sink is open and a warm breeze flutters the curtains and I can hear geese out on the lake. For a moment it doesn't matter if this is First Lisa or Second Lisa. Besides, if you go looking for subtle changes in somebody (or somebody's photographs), aren't you apt to find them, since people are changing all the time? But this is different, this thing with Lisa. It's not just her writing that has changed but her speaking, too, her words.

Take the Murakami quip, for instance. It's not that she would be unfamiliar with his obsession—or should I say his narrators' obsession—but it's just not something she'd say. Because saying it suggests some sort of admiration or respect, and Murakami is not a writer she admires or respects. (Lisa holds an unorthodox theory that Murakami is not really Japanese.) There is no bite, no sarcasm to *not a Murakami girl?* Her question hangs there in the air, as if she's been caught out and the best I can do is pretend I don't notice and fill the silence with a quip back. But before I can . . .

We should have come alone, she says, tightening her grip around my waist.

However, we've never come here before without

Marin. We have never even talked about it. But I want to see where this leads.

Right, left her with Fernie, I say.

Fernie is Lisa's sister, adored by Marin in the way girls sometimes adore their aunts.

Fernie who never cuts her hair, Lisa says.

It's true, Fernie's hair is down to her waist and I wonder what the connection is between that and Lisa's new look.

Left Marin with Fernie for a good long time, she says. How would that suit you?

How *would* that suit me, I wonder. I don't know if it's luck but I play my next card just right. I turn around, look Lisa in her green eyes, which seem so flat now framed by her new short bangs, and say, How would that suit *Fernie*, is the question.

Who cares what Fernie thinks? How would being alone here without Marin suit you? she asks.

I don't understand what sort of water we've waded into here but whatever it is it's not the sort of water we've been in before. I realize suddenly that Marin has been a part of us from the day she arrived; we've literally not been apart from her except when she's at school. Twelve years of marriage, eight of them with the three of us, the balance thrown from two people to three. And if the gait of the horse changed with Marin's arrival, we seem to have adapted just fine, so smoothly in fact that I never noticed the shifted gait until just now, with Lisa's question about being here without Marin.

Then I realize that I don't know where Marin is. She had gone into town with Lisa but Lisa's dramatic return with the new haircut distracted me. Then I hear it, the shattering glass, the scream. Coming from the greenhouse.

15.

Between Marin's shriek and my arrival at the greenhouse, some thirty or forty seconds elapse, but each one lasts so long. You imagine the worst, of course, your child all cut up and bleeding, her insides reversed. You picture her sprawled and drooling on her back on the cracked cement, with watering hoses around her in grotesque, snake-like patterns, the shattered glass from the roof in triangular shards on and around her body like in a diorama of some obscure religious ritual. And then, oddly, you think of tomorrow, a tomorrow without Marin. She is going to turn eight someday and you imagine her birthday without her, and will you still get that electronic birthday greeting from your insurance man, which was always strange anyway, him sending a birthday greeting to your daughter's email, as if.

Some of what I imagine is true. A pane of glass has indeed fallen from the greenhouse ceiling, shattering into unreckonable geometric shapes. But Marin is unhurt and I am so full of light that I notice but don't register that she's got a fresh haircut, too, short like her mom's. She is crying, standing there with her arms to her sides as if by moving she'll cause another plate of glass to break free. The first thing she says is Daddy, be careful! I pick her up into my arms, feeling slightly heroic, and carry her out to where Lisa meets us in the yard, the color drained from her face. Oh, baby, she says, as I pass Marin over. As she carries her up to the cottage I turn back and reenter the greenhouse, thinking about what Marin said about Lisa's secret book. Is that what Marin was doing there, looking for it?

The light in the greenhouse is creamy, somehow.

Looking up, I see the space where the glass pane is missing and wonder what finally caused it to fall and if others will follow. There's not much here. A few rows of long wooden tables, the defunct watering-system hoses, stacks of black plastic growing pots of various sizes. The back wall isn't glass like the rest of the place, but rather loose plastic, swaying in the breeze. As I approach it I see a wooden crate with a gray hose coming out from a crude hole on top and beside it another crate with a similar hole but no hose. The top looks askew and I know what I'm going to find before I even remove it, except that it's not a notebook like I imagined but a black three-ring binder with a pink notecard Scotch-taped to the front. *Kristy and Marlene: A Play.*

It's funny, the first thing I feel is pride that Lisa's written something new and I don't think twice about opening it because, after all, Marin already has. The ten pages are printed out in that old familiar dot-matrix type. You can actually see the tiny dots that make up the letters. I should first say that the Lisa computer has been moved up to the room where Lisa writes, which explains the dot matrix printouts in the greenhouse. By Lisa for Lisa. I smile. I only dimly made the connection between the names before. Hadn't Jobs named the computer after his daughter, and then denied it? A quick glance at one of the scenes tells me that, no doubt, we are dealing with another Lisa here, not the Lisa writer I married, who would never include dialogue like this:

KRISTY: Do you want me to come in or not?
MARLENE: Of course I do. Don't be so sensitive.
KRISTY: Look who's talking.
MARLENE: Fine then, don't come in. Just stand out there in the cold.
KRISTY: Marly, you have to fucking press it.
MARLENE: I am pressing it.

A distant, deep rumble from offstage, like thunder slowed down.

KRISTY: . . .
MARLENE: . . .
KRISTY: So, you say you want me to come in but you won't let me come in. What, is there a secret password or something?
MARLENE: . . .
MARLENE: . . .
MARLENE: Wrecan.

And then there is the doodle, a wolf in black and red ink, standing on its hind legs, its front paws up like hands except with claws tipped in blood from some other dimension. Over the drawing, in an arc, are the cartoonish words Too Hot to Handle.

There is something about the wolf's eyes that terrifies.

They seem to be spinning.

16.

How to play it with Lisa? How to play it with Marin? These are the questions. The questions of the moment. I'm back in the house.

Marin is just scared more than anything, Lisa says from halfway down the stairs. I tucked her in for a nap. She pushes up one of the sleeves of her black wool sweater and looks unbalanced.

Is the greenhouse the same age as the cottage? I ask her.

She laughs and takes another step down the stairs.

You'd have had to ask my dead aunt, she says. It's funny, Lisa never refers to her aunt by her name.

But since I can't, I say.

The greenhouse was here first, so it must be older, she says. When they brought me here as a girl there was no house. She takes a step closer to me.

No house?

Another step.

Nope, she says.

Step.

Just the greenhouse?

Step.

Right.

So your aunt and uncle bought the land with the greenhouse, and then built the house?

They must have.

Were there ever any plants in it? I mean live plants?

Dead plants can be *alive*, too, Lisa says.

Before I go on I should come back to Lisa's fascination with Zora Neale Hurston, not the novelist Hurston known for *Their Eyes Were Watching God*, but the anthropologist Hurston who wrote *Tell My Horse: Voodoo and Life in Haiti and Jamaica*, a remarkable book from 1938 that includes the first known photograph of a zombie. This had been the subject of Lisa's master's thesis—how Hurston's book had provided the urtext for the Hollywood zombie movie craze of the '40s, especially *I Walked with a Zombie*. But it was an urtext that was perverted by the white-culture industry, as Lisa called it, which racialized zombies as the radical Other (I'm using Lisa's language here). This is the passage Lisa had photocopied and pinned above her desk in grad school, describing how the making of a zombie begins:

> Maybe a plantation owner has come to the Bocor to "buy" some laborers, or perhaps an enemy wants the utmost in revenge. He makes an agreement with the Bocor to do the work. After the proper ceremony, the Bocor in his most powerful and dreaded aspect mounts a horse with his face toward the horse's tail and rides after dark to the house of the victim. There he places his lips to the crack of the door and sucks out the soul of the victim and rides off in all speed.

She even called me Bocor for a while, before Marin came, back when things like that didn't feel jinxed, because after Marin we were so much more careful about what forces might creep into our little family.

But back to now: Lisa's at the bottom of the stairs. She closer-stills herself to me.

The plants were carnivorous, she says.

Her breath smells minty. It takes me a second to put it together.

The flies and beetles and moths weren't large enough, she says, so I had to feed them field mice. It's hard to believe she'd ask a child to do this but there you go, that's my aunt.

Plants eat mice?

These ones did, she says.

I can hardly believe it, but I don't want to break the spell. It's like the pre-Marin days when we first met and how clearly I remember that it was Lisa who made the first move. Seeing how awkward and self-conscious I was, she put her hand on my leg in the movie theater and then I put my hand on top of hers. What was the movie? One of the *Mad Max* movies I'm pretty sure and there was something exotic and romantic about the vast Australian deserts and the freedom and the movement. A feeling of expansive sandswept loneliness that somehow extended to us, too, canceling out the hope of ever feeling connected to anyone except each other. As still as our bodies were in that theater, our hearts were racing.

What's got you all riled? she asks.

Has she ever used that phrase before? Now I'm overthinking things because once you go looking for changes in someone, you're bound to find them, right? Her arms are around my neck and we're closer now, our bodies touching, and I notice that Lisa is looking not at me but at something just behind me. If there's any such thing as an expectant look then that's what she's got in her eyes, which have widened a little bit and are almost pouring out green. I can feel the green, feel it seeping into me and

I pull away from her and swivel around to see what it is she's looking at and catch a glimpse of it in the kitchen, something in the shape of a kite. The outline of a kite, as if drawn in pencil in the air, hovering there above the counter. The outline vibrates, like something animated, and then disappears.

What the hell, Lisa? I say.

I know, she says. I've seen it before. There's something wrong with this place. It changes things. That's why I brought us here.

She opens her eyes wide. Guh-guh-girls just want to have fun, she says.

17.

What Lisa says she means by that (not the guh-girls part) is that it's good for us to come here, as a family, to get away from city life and be in nature, where we can recharge and just spend time together. But I wonder. After all, *it changes things* has a fairly sinister ring to it, and the fact that she said she'd seen the kite-thing before and hadn't mentioned it is also strange. But before I get ahead of myself I should say something about the kitchen door, the one I hadn't noticed until the other day. It's easy to see why I missed it, not only because it's half-covered by the sideboard but also because it's on a wall of old knotty pine, the outline of the doorframe blending in with the wood. And yet, how *could* I have missed it, having walked by it hundreds of times over the years?

I pull the sideboard back, scraping it across the linoleum floor.

The door is a bit undersized, the sort of closet or basement door you find in old houses like this, houses built before everything was supersized. It's got a small wooden knob like the ones on the cupboards and when I give it a gentle pull the door opens. But not into much. It's a shallow space behind the door, no more than a foot deep, and propped within that narrow space is what first appears to be the back of a large frame that might hold a painting. Written on the brown-paper backing in dark ink are the words DO NOT REVERSE. I kneel down and reach out with both hands to lift the frame, but it's heavier than expected. It's a heavy-gravitied old mirror, the type you might find attached to the back of a dresser, and not a painting. I rap on it with my knuckles and it's hard.

DO NOT REVERSE.

Does that mean don't turn it around?

The writing is bold and cautiously neat. Maybe the writing is the original instructions for assembly, as if someone would attach a mirror facing the wrong way on a dresser. Or maybe someone—Aunt Elle?—wrote this and hid the mirror here, although what kind of hiding place is this?

It's the hiding place of something that wants to be found, I think.

Just on the other side of the frame, on the floor, is what appears to be a shard of glass, or perhaps a fragment from the mirror itself, coated in a light dust. It would be easy for me to reach down and pick up the shard, but I hesitate. Instead, I fish out a small flashlight from the kitchen junk drawer and why I do what I do next I'm not sure. Even though I can hear Lisa and Marin out in the garden, I still look over my shoulder as I squat down before the open door, as if what I'm doing is somehow taboo.

The shard isn't lying flat but at an angle that I'm hoping will allow my light to reflect off it and onto the mirror so that I can at least confirm that it is in fact a mirror and not a painting or something else. It's difficult to see but there it is, a mirror, reflected back in the glass shard. A wave of nausea overtakes me, a feeling of vertigo. I think about bullying my way in with my hand but pause instead.

What's reflected in the reversed mirror doesn't make sense.

What I catch a glimpse of is a forest, as if that's what the mirror is facing. I think it's this disorientation that makes me feel sick and I drop the flashlight behind the door and it flickers off and rolls away. Before I can reach in for it, I hear them coming up to the cottage from the garden, Lisa and Marin, and so I shut the door and move the sideboard back. I'm unsteady on my feet and Lisa notices.

What's wrong, you're sweating, she says, holding a bunch of wildflowers in her hand. Marin trails in behind her with another bunch, clutched to her chest. She's got on that crazy dress Lisa's mom got her, the one I thought they threw out. For a moment I see double from the dizziness: two Lisas, two Marins. Then Lisa says something that doesn't sound like Lisa at all: The garden is all wildflowers now. Soon everything will be.

What about this sounds so off that it scares me? Why does it sound like a wish or, worse, a threat? There is some detached flatness in her voice. And when Lisa says it, she's not even looking at me but beyond me, at the door. Does she know about the door? Can she see it? Has she ever opened it? As usual, Marin breaks the spell.

Daddy, vases!

For the flowers, I assume she means, and with that my focus readjusts and the wave of nausea dissipates. Lisa is already reaching up into one of the high cupboards, then bringing down two old, blue-glass vases.

Let me fill them, Marin says, stepping up onto the stool in front of the sink.

What a day, Lisa says. We saw a fox, didn't we, Marin?

With a baby rabbit, Marin says, focused on filling the vases with water.

In its mouth, Lisa mouths to me, with a wink.

The fox was carrying it because it couldn't hop, Marin says. He was saving it.

18.

Marin and Lisa are napping so I go up to Lisa's office. I tell myself I'm going to check if she has enough paper for that old dot-matrix printer or if I need to scutter around for some more in the undersized storage room beneath the stairs.

But I'm really there to check on Lisa, the other Lisa.

I have to admit, she has got the computer set up nicely on her oak desk in front of the open window overlooking the front lot and I'm struck by the bulkiness of the keyboard and the clunky square mouse. I am seized with surprise that it still works and that Lisa is using it to write new plays.

But that's the question, isn't it?

Who is using whom?

What's that saying by Thoreau? "We do not ride upon the railroad; it rides upon us."

I have to admit, the shape of the computer comes across as off-putting, verging on menacing, but maybe that's just because I came of age with the model that followed, the classic Macintosh. The Lisa 2 is a flattened version of this, though version is not the right word since the Lisa came first, so in a way the Mac is an iteration of the Lisa. In any case, the breadbox shape is, like I said, menacing, if not sleekly obscene, as if it expects something. What's it waiting for? I wonder, as I stand there in the doorway. That's when I begin to put two and two together, that Lisa's plays began changing once she started using the Lisa.

And as I stand there thinking this, it's almost as if Lisa acknowledges my hunch because the computer's edges—for just a second—assume the same wavery vibration as the kite outline. It lasts only a moment, gone after I blink, but long enough for me to notice. I shut my eyes and picture Lisa sitting there typing away, her fingers directed to write scenes she would never write otherwise, using words she would never use, like fucking as in "Marly, you have to fucking press it." These are not her words, because Lisa is a classicist and if anything her plays are closer to Eugene O'Neill than to Caryl Churchill, sorry to say.

I think about sabotaging the Lisa 2 or disarming it somehow, like by damaging the power cord, but of course I don't, because I'm curious to see what else Lisa will come up with. The truth is I'm not ready to escalate yet, and if there is anything I've learned from my interactions with clients on their reiterations, it's *don't be the one to make the first move*. So I just stand there and observe. I can see why Lisa likes writing in this spot, with its elemental wide-planked wooden floor and those thin, yellow drapes like a faded nightgown framing the window. When I turn to leave I hear something, a gentle rustle of paper from her desk?

It must just be a breeze from the window, I think, and don't bother to look back.

19.

I'm on my way to the village the next morning because Mel wants to talk again. Since we can't meet in person, he is sending someone in his stead, which is unusual but not unheard of. I find my way back to that narrow forest road Marin and I got lost on and spot the tree with the K+M carving. It's a beautiful spot with the morning sun dappling the trees and the heavy green moss that clumps in soft mounds throughout this region. I've stopped here to get a picture of the carving with my phone and while I'm taking it I hear a high-pitched yipping in the distance. I've heard coyotes before and that's what this sounds like except it's followed by another call, one that sounds more like a howl than a yip. Are there wolves in this part of the world? Un-wolves? I don't think so, and for all I know, coyotes make that same sustained howl.

I hear it again, closer now, and can't help but think of what Marin said about Lisa's wolf doodles. I'm almost embarrassed as I make my way back to the car with a bit more speed than usual. Like, what, a werewolf in some Nazi uniform is going to ambush me? Like that vulgar scene in *An American Werewolf in London*, a scene that seriously disturbed me when I saw it the first time.

But it's okay to be scared, I tell myself, some mantra I picked up from a self-care podcast. By the time I reach the village the fear has subsided. My thoughts turn to Mel, who's been so troublesome and yet who pays so very well. His reiteration is not complete yet and if that's what this meeting is about I'm going to have to hold firm. Or *hold tight*, as my therapist used to say, which I always thought was odd advice, more like something my Calvinist grandfather would counsel, rather than a therapist. As if holding tight would make my problems disappear!

I park in the shaded lot across the street from the ice-cream shop and make my way to the park with the reflecting pool and a modern sculpture that appears to represent three children sitting on a curb with their heads down between their knees, as if dejected, or even weeping. I choose a bench on the park's far side, the unsettling sculpture obscured by a small stand of trees. From here I can see the main entrance to the park off Buttonwood Avenue, and as a group of people enter, one of them peels away and heads in my direction, a short, stocky man not really dressed for this warm weather. As he approaches I see him dabbing his forehead with a white handkerchief, which he then stuffs into the breast pocket of his brown blazer.

Oh, dear, he says, gripping my hand. I seem to have overdressed.

I'm immediately relieved. He's sort of a nerd; I have nothing to fear. Why was I worried Mel would send some monstrous, towering figure to further negotiate his reiterations fee? The stocky man maneuvers his way closer and takes a seat next to me on the bench and pulls out a comb, one of those black plastic ones, and runs it through his thinning hair, which seems damp from sweat.

These days, these days, he mutters, and I think he's referring to the heat, or maybe to just the general condition of his life, or the world. In any case, he continues: Mel thanks you for meeting him . . . er . . . for meeting me, on his behalf, under these unlikely circumstances. I suppose, well, I suppose you know he's a bit concerned about your progress—no insult or malignment intended—on the procedure.

Reiteration, I correct him.

Pardon?

Reiteration. I prefer that term.

Of course, he says. Oh my, I didn't mean to offend . . .

No offense taken. So, what's Mel's concern? I don't have much time.

(I have all the time in the world, of course.)

Well, he says. His fingers flutter a bit and he rubs his palms down the front of his pants.

If it's about the payment schedule . . .

Oh no, no, he says. He seems to have broken out in a sweat again and stands up, his arms extended out in front of him, as if searching for something in the air.

This heat, he exclaims, and at this time of year!

Feel free to take off your jacket, I tell him.

Oh, thank you, he says, as if the thought hadn't occurred to him. Beneath his jacket he wears a TV-weatherman yellow oxford shirt about to burst at the buttons. The shirt is completely soaked.

I'm afraid Mel's concerns are more . . . structural.

Go on, I say.

The man seems to have gained some confidence and, returning to the park bench, looks directly at me for the first time.

Well, he's fuzzy on the tapering part.

Mel and I already went over that. It's a standard part of the reiteration.

And this is something that can't be changed? he asks.

Not without compromising the process itself, no.

Which, I'm to understand, you haven't begun yet.

It will be done by the agreed-upon date. You can leave the procedural details up to me.

Oh, dear, it's not me, he says. I'm only here on behalf of Mel.

Okay then, you can tell Mel that he can leave the procedural details up to me.

This quiets him for a moment and there is a deep peace in the park. If there are overlords they have fallen asleep, their evacuated panoptic gaze replaced with peace.

The man—this envoy—seems lost in thought and for a good while we don't speak.

And yet, about that tapering bit, he continues, finally.

So, what exactly is Mel's question? I ask.

Well, he didn't send me with one.

Then why *did* he send you?

To raise the issue of . . . he trails off.

The issue of, I prod him.

The tapering.

Yes, and what about the tapering? I ask. What is the issue about the tapering?

Mel didn't say. I thought *you'd* know.

Well, I don't know, I tell him. I just design the reiteration.

But I've raised the issue, haven't I? he asks. He's almost pleading.

I suppose so, although I don't know what, exactly, the issue is you're raising.

The issue about the tapering process.

Yes, but what about the tapering process?

I suppose the process itself, he says, is the issue.

And as I said, that's not my end of things. Mel knows this. Why are you really here?

This seems to leave him even more flustered than he is already, if that's possible. He stuffs himself back into his blazer—barely—runs his hand across the top of his head, mutters something about being late for another meeting, and zigzags off across the park, glancing back only once as he passes the sad girls sculpture.

20.

It's early morning back at the cottage. We have three days left until we are supposed to go back home. The best thing to do is to forget Lisa's hidden play, but of course trying to forget it just presses it forward in my brain all the more. The main thing is I'm curious if she has added to it since I found it. It's raining hard outside and Marin and I are in the room where the TV is, working on a puzzle of a blue octopus. She is in full concentration mode, in her nightgown, her freckles glowing a little bit. She's on her knees on the chair, leaning forward over the table, holding a puzzle piece in her hand, searching. Yes! she says, fitting it in and pushing it down with her thumb.

Nice one, I say.

Dad, I want to see one before they go extinct, she says.

Is this the first time I'm Dad rather than Daddy?

Shit, I think.

I pretend I don't hear so she'll say it again.

Daddy, an octopus before it goes extinct.

She says this half with words and half with her hands, without even thinking about it, as if this hybrid form of communicating is becoming natural to her, ingrained in who she is and who she is becoming.

They're not going extinct, honey.

Yes, they are. We learned about it in Mrs. Barnes's.

Ah, Mrs. Barnes, a real pencils-down-now doomsayer. Thanks to Mrs. Barnes I have been scolded for letting the tap run while I'm brushing my teeth, flushing the toilet too often, watering the yard *ever*, and not unplugging, at night, various little glowing gadgets around the house. The fact that she's right, of course, makes it only worse. I'm on the side of goodness in this world, even if that goodness comes in the ungainly shape of Mrs. Barnes.

The rain is really pelting this vulnerable cottage now and suddenly the back kitchen door blows open and a gust of cool, wet air sweeps through the room, ruffling Marin's nightgown and even unsettling the ashes in the fireplace. As I move to shut the door, Lisa comes down from upstairs, and in the chaos of the moment I catch a glimpse of her, except it's not her. Of course it's her, it must be, but she's wrong, like a made-up version of herself. It's Lisa but not Lisa. Has she ever been this tall? Have her eyes ever been this wide and far apart, manga-like?

And what is that she clutches to her chest?

A brown envelope like the one that delivered the marked piece of bark, that's what she clutches with drama like she wants me to see it. I reach the door and push it shut against the wind. Marin is crying and in Lisa's arms, and everything resets to normal. I'm actually glad to see Marin crying—it reassures me, somehow.

And then, as suddenly as it began, the rain ends. The sun comes out. I go back and re-open the kitchen door to let fresh air in and tear off some paper towels to dry the floor where the rain came in. I'm feeling generous, expansive, and I suggest we all go to the village for breakfast. This stops Marin's crying and she drops from Lisa and is now in my arms. She puts her hands on my face and pushes down on the tip of my nose.

You look funny, she says.

I push the tip of her nose up and say, Now we both look funny.

To my surprise Lisa comes over and pushes her own nose up and with another finger pulls down one of her eyelids and rolls her eyes back until they're white.

Ve are all vedy funny now, she says.

I remember this because it's our last happy moment together as a family.

21.

A family as I used to know it, I should say.

The changes accelerate after the storm, beginning with a new notebook I discover in the greenhouse. Who is to say Lisa shouldn't have the right to create what she wants, where she wants? If she's working on plays she doesn't want me to see, then that's her right as an autonomous human being. "Union is only possible to those who are units," Margaret Fuller wrote in one of her essays Lisa and I both read in an American-literature survey class we took together as undergrads, the class where we met, actually, taught by Dr. Solomon with his stiff posture and tight red bow ties, whose lectures were so full of surprise we wondered where the class time had gone. This was in the era of the last real wooden podiums and chalkboards and professors who wore button-up shirts.

You could still smoke on the patios of campus buildings and the idea of an occasional small class meeting at a bar raised no eyebrows.

There was no Rate My Professor.

No AI bots writing our papers.

Everything was either word of mouth or a crapshoot, an element of randomness and surprise. Sometimes we even learned more from the sucky professors than from the good and polished ones.

Because they were failures, too, and in their failures we saw glimpses of our own.

And now we'd moved from those scrubby times to these polished, filtered ones.

And here we are.

The new notebook is in the same greenhouse crate as the Marlene notebook. Instead of in a black binder, it's in a red one, and I have more time to read it this time because Lisa and Marin are down at the lake. This one is called *Bloodsport* and unlike Lisa's previous plays it cuts right to it, so to speak. One of the characters is named Marlene here, too; maybe this is the same Marlene. I get the *Night of the Living Dead* and *Memento* references because I'm familiar with Lisa's obsessions.

BOBBY: It's what you wanted, right?
MARLENE: If you let me go, you know what's gonna happen.
BOBBY: That's why I'm not going to let you go.

Thunder from offstage. The walls go red. Bobby is distracted.

MARLENE: "They're coming to get you, Barbara."

BOBBY: You paid me to do this to you, so let me do it.

MARLENE: Why should I make it easy? I want my money's worth.

BOBBY: So, what, you're one of the Sad Girls all of a sudden? You paid me for a job and now, predictably, you're trying to talk your way out it. Next thing you know, you'll be asking me to put down my hammer.

Another roll of thunder. The walls go deeper red.

MARLENE: Maybe you should take a look in the basement.
BOBBY: Why would I do that?
MARLENE: To see what you've done.

Bobby steps closer with the hammer.

BOBBY: I've never been here before. I've never been in the basement.
MARLENE: Are you sure? Think about it. How did you know how to find this place?
BOBBY: You told me how to get here.
MARLENE: Did I?
BOBBY: That was part of the agreement. You texted me instructions, directions. You told me how to find the cottage, where to find the hammer.
MARLENE: And what to do with it.
BOBBY: That, too.
MARLENE: Unless you go into the basement again.
BOBBY: *Again*? I've never been there once so I can't go again.
MARLENE: Why don't you go down and see for yourself if you've been there before? I've unlocked the basement door for you. You can take your hammer.
BOBBY: But that's not what you paid me for. That's not part of the agreement.
MARLENE: Then let's change the agreement.
BOBBY: We can't change the agreement. That's part of the agreement.
MARLENE: So, it's fate then. It's determined.
BOBBY: It's what you wanted and I'm here to do it.

MARLENE: So, a girl can't change her mind?
BOBBY: You can change your mind but it won't change what I'm gonna do.

There is more but I hear Marin's laughter and just as I put the binder back in the crate she bounds into the greenhouse, her orange beach towel around her neck. She runs so fast her sandals come off.

Be careful of the glass, I shout, meeting her halfway as she jumps into my arms. Her hair is wet and cold. Lisa appears in the doorway in her bikini and she looks so beautiful. Her wet, short hair. I just want to hold the image and the moment and, for a few seconds, it sticks. No one moves. Marin's in my arms, her head on my shoulder, Lisa's in the doorway, as still as can be, and the sun's coming in through the glass roof, a brighter square of it on the floor beneath where the pane fell earlier.

The sickly phone ringing in its brown tones from the cottage breaks the spell. It rings and rings and by the time we reach the kitchen it's still ringing. Lisa answers it, listens for a few moments. I hear a faint voice on the line. Lisa hangs up.

Who was it? I ask.

Nobody, she says. There was no one there.

22.

It's a hot night—the hottest yet of the summer—and the windows are all open. We're sleeping without covers, and the moonlight coming in through our bedroom window gives everything a sort of soft, blue metallic glow.

Lisa's breathing steadily beside me but I can't sleep. I'm thinking about Mel and what his sweaty representative in the park said about the tapering part of the reiteration. Of all the elements, why would Mel be concerned about that? It's hardly the most important part, and yet for some clients, well, it's just difficult for them to get their heads around it. I suppose it's because it involves a level of contradiction that is too vast to comprehend. The tapering, a sort of diminishing that seems impossible, is really the easiest part of the process, and yet one that trips up clients like Mel.

But the very idea that Mel sent the sweaty man worries me.

That's what's keeping me awake.

A client like Mel can present downstream problems. After all, it was Mel with his *check this out* casualness that drew me back into the process in the first place. Mel and his rupees, Mel and his millions. The thing people like Mel don't know is that I don't need to do anything to model their reiterations because, for God's sake, that's what reiterations are. It amazes and frightens me that they can't, or won't, see this simple fact. The truth is, I finished Mel's reiteration within hours of finalizing the contract and that's all part of it, the mystique. I worked hard early on to perfect the process, so building that labor-cost into recent ones like Mel's makes sense. At least to me.

And so, I wonder: was the sweaty envoy-man really there on Mel's behalf to talk about tapering, or was he there for some other, darker reason? In my line of business you can't be too careful, and yet careful is the last thing I am lately. Why did I let him shake my hand? Why was his grip so strong? I get out of bed, go into the bathroom, shut the door, and turn on the light, holding my palms out in front of me. Which hand did he shake? My right one. There, in the webby part between my thumb and index finger, is a small, circular discolored spot, like a tiny purple stain. I rub it and it feels like a cat's rough tongue, not skin-like. I hold it closer to my face and see little spikes or shoots extending from the circle; it looks like an asterisk. But what is it?

My briefcase is down in the kitchen and so I set up the small Mead-Fancher reader on the table and pour myself half a glass of milk. I unfasten the metal case it's in, something like an old typewriter carrier. It's an archaic-looking thing, like a vintage radio with silver knobs, two round screens each about the diameter of a golf ball, a delicate gold-foil antenna, and a lens-focused Gaussian beam. There is a little green metal oil can strapped to the inside of the case and I squeeze a few drops of oil onto the thin wires that connect the input and reader screens. It's one of the early models, repurposed for what I'm about to use it for now.

Although I try to ignore it, there it is, the obscure gray line from the Zora Neale Hurston photo (the Hurston line, I think of it as) floating there before my eyes. Actually, that's what it feels like: a floater, one of those squigglies you have in your eyes, except the line doesn't move. It seems to be floating, but not moving, hanging in the air between me and the Mead-Fancher reader. I just ignore it. I don't need something else to worry about right now.

The power of the little machine resides not so much in what it's able to detect, as in its invisibility: no one knows it exists (well, except for Marin), and so no one can avoid or elude it. You can't defend against what you don't know. I plug it in and there is a snap and a hiss and that familiar, somehow comforting, ozone smell. I place my wrist in the armature and position my hand so the discolored spot falls between the two green light beams. Then: a faint flutter, a signal, on the screens, enough to tell me that the mark's not organic. Unfortunately, that's about all I learn, but it's enough to know that the sweaty man was sweaty only because that's the easiest way to make these little devices stick.

23.

It's around this time that I begin to wonder: what if Lisa is not changing into something new, but reverting to something old? What if she's not evolving, but regressing to the person she was before I met her in that class on those Transcendentalist writers? When you first meet someone, you're meeting them for who they are, and for when they are. As I'm thinking this, back upstairs in bed after the Gaussian reading, Lisa begins to talk in her sleep. The house is perfect, she mumbles, and then, as clear as day, she says, Don't do it, Dan. There is an alarm to her voice and it's so clear and direct that for a moment it feels as if she's talking directly to me, and has mistaken me for someone named Dan.

Oh Dan, no! she whispers.

It's okay, I say, in the dark. It's just a dream.

Be quiet, he'll hear you, she says, panicky.

It's 2:00 a.m. and I can't get back to sleep. I leave Lisa to her dreaming and head downstairs and when I flick on the kitchen light I see two things, almost at the same time. The wavy, shimmering outline of the kite, and the door behind the sideboard, which has been cracked open. The kite outline hovers above the sink and, sort of like a floater in your eye, moves when you try to focus on it. I glance at the secret door and then back to the kite and it's gone. As I move towards the door, something else happens. I feel a cool breeze, as if the small door has opened to the outside night. I also see a dim light coming from within the narrow space behind the door and for a moment I freeze, until I realize that it must be the flashlight I dropped earlier. It must have come back on. The draft is stronger as I approach and there's also the scent of the outdoors, of the outdoors at night, like wet ferns, I think. But, of course, there is no outside behind the door, just that damned mirror, the shard of glass, and, apparently, my flashlight.

It's not possible that the door has opened by itself and I'm overtaken with the sudden fear that someone's in the cottage. I check the doors: locked. And then it occurs to me that someone else *is* in the cottage, two someones. And then it's clear: Lisa has opened the door. I only have to think back to when she and Marin came in with the flowers and the way Lisa's gaze drifted just over my shoulder, to the door. There in the kitchen I have to make a decision: do I reach in for the flashlight or just close the door, push the sideboard back, and forget about it? That's the sensible thing to do but there's something about that flashlight being on, burning away behind a closed door, that makes me uncomfortable. There's no question anymore: I need to retrieve the flashlight.

I move the sideboard, giving myself more space, and kneel down. DO NOT REVERSE. Again, I wonder, who would write a thing like that? What does it mean? It's an instruction, clearly, but when you think about it, it doesn't quite make sense. Doesn't "reverse" mean to go backwards? Or maybe it does make sense, and is just another way of saying DO NOT TURN AROUND. That would be even more frightening, because it suggests that the person reading it not turn around. I spin through all these options in my head but it's my first instinct I stick with: DO NOT REVERSE means DO NOT TURN THIS MIRROR AROUND.

And why would I? Other than with my reiterations (which, after all, are my job!) I'm not one to court danger. I reach in for the flashlight, my shoulder pressed against the door frame, bracing for a wave of nausea that doesn't come. I feel the flashlight with my fingers, and as I touch it I hear something behind me, in the kitchen. I grab the flashlight and turn around, and there's Marin.

Daddy, I can't sleep, she says.

It's okay, I tell her, softly closing the door.

I pick her up in my arms and think she might be sleepwalking because she doesn't mention the door or even ask what I'm doing.

As I carry her back upstairs she whispers, Old MacDonald?

I sing it to her softly as I lay her back

into her bed and pull up the covers. I think about my own father soothing me to sleep when I was a child, after Mom died. It's something I haven't told Marin yet, about her grandmother. We've called it an accident, what happened to her. It's not just the suicide, but details of the suicide, and how telling Marin the truth will lead to questions about these details. I don't want to have to answer the question *How did she do it?* And yet if we wait too long to tell her, will Marin view it as a betrayal? *You lied to me!*

Thankfully, with my network, I can scrub the details of her death clean, so it's not like Marin could easily discover what actually happened. But what did actually happen? I was twelve when she died, when we were still living on the hops farm in the Upper Peninsula. From the loft of our barn, looking out over Lake Superior that spring, you could see where the Edmund Fitzgerald sank off Whitefish Point. That's where I was when the screaming came, and then the smoke. Did I choke on the fumes of my own mother burning below me, in the hay? Did I hear her call my name before she lit the match, as if to say *You couldn't save me in time, could you? You weren't fast enough. Or was it that you didn't care enough, that you were somehow glad to see me go, and so you waited?*

No, I can't tell Marin that part, not ever. That infernus shall remain lidded.

Not even Lisa knows.

But could I have intervened, could I have stopped her? It's strange how memory works, not just memory, but our memories of memories. When I think of the day it happened—and the actual moment I smelled the smoke from below the loft—am I remembering the moment itself, or subsequent memories of the moment?

Marin is soon asleep and as I leave her room I crack the door open the way she likes it. The cottage is so quiet now I can hear my own heartbeat. I crawl back into bed with Lisa and don't wake until morning.

24.

Early morning, I should say. 4:30 early. Why do I slip out of bed and grab the flashlight to sneak out to the greenhouse? Because I want to see if Lisa has added more to the *Bloodsport* play, whose lines I've been running over in my head since I read them, as if I am rehearsing for a part in it. The greenhouse is cool and quiet in the moonlight. The notebook is there, but in a slightly different position. Lisa has been writing.

> *The phone rings. Marlene answers it, listens for a few seconds, then hangs up.*
>
> BOBBY: Who was it?
> MARLENE: Nobody.
> BOBBY: I heard someone.
> MARLENE: There was no one to hear.
> BOBBY: Then who called?
> MARLENE: The phone rang. I picked it up. There was nobody on the line. What do you want me to say?
> BOBBY: You can start by telling me who it was, or . . .
> MARLENE: Or what?
> BOBBY: Or I can star-69 it.

MARLENE: Sure, go ahead . . .

She holds out the phone.

MARLENE: . . . but be careful.
BOBBY: Of?
MARLENE: What you might conjure.
BOBBY: You think that's the best way to scare me? With your voodoo threats?

Bobby presses the call-back numbers and listens. The sound as he presses the numbers is live. The audience hears what he hears. Something hissing, like a boiler or a radiator steaming. He holds the phone out away from his ear, as if to share the sound with Marlene.

BOBBY: What's this, some trick?
MARLENE: Like I said, there's no one there.
BOBBY: But there's *some*thing.
MARLENE: It's just the line, Bobby, the static from the line.
BOBBY: *From the line*? What is this, the '70s?

What to make of these parched words that echo our own back-and-forth from just the other day?

Who was it?

Nobody.

Had my scripturient Lisa already incorporated our conversation into her play? I'd like to think, no, of course not. This is just a coincidence. There must be dozens—maybe more—of plays or plots featuring someone answering a phone and lying about who's on the other end. Deceit is the stuff of drama and, after all, Lisa's the writer, not me. Although, to be fair, my reiterations are also a form of creativity, of storytelling, and in fact the reiterations what I work on when I come back from the greenhouse.

It's still early and dark outside.

I open the small briefcase and set up the Mead-Fancher reader on the kitchen table, this time in its holographic-mode setting, which takes a little time. It's a delicate operation, always the most difficult and harrowing part of the procedure. My hands are not as steady as they used to be and the stylus is very sensitive, so I have to hold it and move it delicately. Bringing the hologram into its proper dimension is really an intuitive process and in Mel's case fairly straightforward, because the data he's given to me is clean and unbroken. The sweaty envoy-man's nonsense about the tapering makes me smile because, really, that's the easiest part. For Mel's reiteration I'm to replace a short meeting from a decade ago with an overlay that changes just one gesture: I'm to eliminate the handshake and replace it with a nod. Apparently, the handshake between Mel and whomever it was he was meeting—let's call her Miss Aitch—signified something more formal to Miss Aitch than to Mel. She took the handshake to be a formal agreement, which it wasn't, Mel told me as part of his instructions for the procedure.

I hear the first murmuration of pine warblers outside, always a sad sound, and continue sketching with the stylus, bringing the hologram into focus and inserting into it the parallel time line that runs in the background across the oval monitor. I keep a circle of wax paper taped over the monitor because it's too bright and the light-level knob broke ages ago. This reiteration is just under seven seconds long, with no preamble or epilogue, although I didn't share this fact with Mel when I quoted him my fee. The natural gestures are always the most challenging part, something that was easier to pull off when my hands were steadier. Removing the handshake is straightforward; replacing it with a nod is the tricky part. Because this is Mel, and because he sent the sweaty man for a visit, I'm more careful about the rendering than normal, making sure the waveforms are intricate and patterned. This will ensure a smooth interface so the reiteration, once it's activated, will replace the original handshake without any memory triggers at all. That's why I'm the best at this, to be honest, because it takes more than just skill to pull off a job like this so smoothly and without alerting the other party, in this case Miss Aitch. It takes imagination.

By the time the sun is up I'm done. This reiteration didn't even involve tapering, since the original gesture was so distinct, though of course I won't tell the sweaty man that if he asks about it again. I close and latch the Mead-Fancher reader back into its case and take it to the trunk of the car and when I come back in I hear Marin stirring upstairs. I fudgel around the kitchen and make some coffee and put the tea kettle on for Lisa. By the time the water is boiling, Mel's job will have been completed and all the consequences that flowed from that handshake will have been removed from history.

25.

At breakfast Lisa says she thinks we should stay here another few days. I've heated the vegan sausage in the same pan I used for the eggs and, because the old toaster is broken, I put the bread in there, too. Marin is already out back looking for butterflies, and the morning sun falls on the kitchen table in such a fake, geometric way.

Are you on a roll? I ask.

Exactly, Lisa says. She's really wolfing down breakfast and I pour her more tea.

The Paul and Julia one?

Yes, except I took your advice and made it less like *Who's Afraid of Virginia Woolf*? and I introduced a knife into the plot, which means . . .

It has to be used, I say.

Right, she says, but unlike a gun, a knife could be used for something harmless. Like cutting open a grapefruit.

But don't you think it's more interesting to use a knife, in a play, to cut open a person rather than a grapefruit?

Depends on what sort of play we're talking about.

Or what sort of person, she says.

This is when it becomes clear that, for the sake of the family, I need to do something about Lisa, the other Lisa, the one upstairs on her desk.

Or at least *I* could stay a few more days, she says, picking up the thread from earlier. In a week I'd be sitting on a good draft, and Marin seems to be getting bored. She misses her friends. School starts in two weeks, so if I stay up here and keep at it one more week I can be back in time to take her to orientation and get her school supplies.

I see, I tell her.

It just feels like I'm on a roll, she says, finishing her eggs. Would you mind?

Of course not. Are you sure Marin would be okay with it?

It would do her good to be away from me for a while. Have you noticed lately how she argues with everything I say? Last night after I read her bedtime story I pointed out how full the moon was and she said, *That's not the real moon.*

Some imagination, just like her mom.

I clear the dishes and pour Lisa another cup of tea.

That's how Marin runs, I say. Hot and cold. Do you remember last Halloween when she insisted I dress up as "Dad" because I wasn't acting like Dad anymore?

Sort of heartbreaking, right? Lisa says.

So, you think the ribbon cartridge will last you through the week? I'm not sure you can even get those anymore.

There are unopened boxes in the stairs closet. I'm good, she says.

And then, almost as if she's reading my mind, Lisa says: You know, it's strange, when I'm up there writing it's like I don't even have to think about it, it just flows, which I always thought was a cliché. It hasn't felt like this since college. I'm thinking it's the keyboard, silly as that sounds. Like it's the spacing between the keys that makes it easier for my fingers to move and so I just sit there and everything comes so easy. It feels like the words are right there just a split second before I think of them. If I read something to that effect in a *Paris Review* interview or whatever, I'd think, Bullshit!

Why bullshit? I ask.

Because normally there's nothing romantic about writing, like we've talked about. But this is different, it really is sort of magical. My aunt would have called it witchy.

I did notice a Ouija board in the closet.

Did I ever tell you about the time she lost it during *The Wizard of Oz?* I used to stay here as a kid during the divorce, and one time, I must have been around Marin's age, she got really sick during the movie. It was in the other room, on the same TV that's there right now, and she went to the bathroom for the longest time. Later she said it was from bad 7UP and for a long time I didn't drink pop of any kind because I worried it might have gone bad. I didn't know any better! But then later, one time when I was a teenager and painted my nails black, she grabbed my hand and I saw the same fear on her face as I had seen during the wicked-witch scene. I don't remember what she said but it doesn't matter. I guess I have always associated those two events and they feel continuous somehow, even though they're separated by years.

Marin is stirring upstairs. I have a sudden fear that she will go into Lisa's office and start playing with the Lisa computer and that the the same spell that's infecting Lisa will infect her.

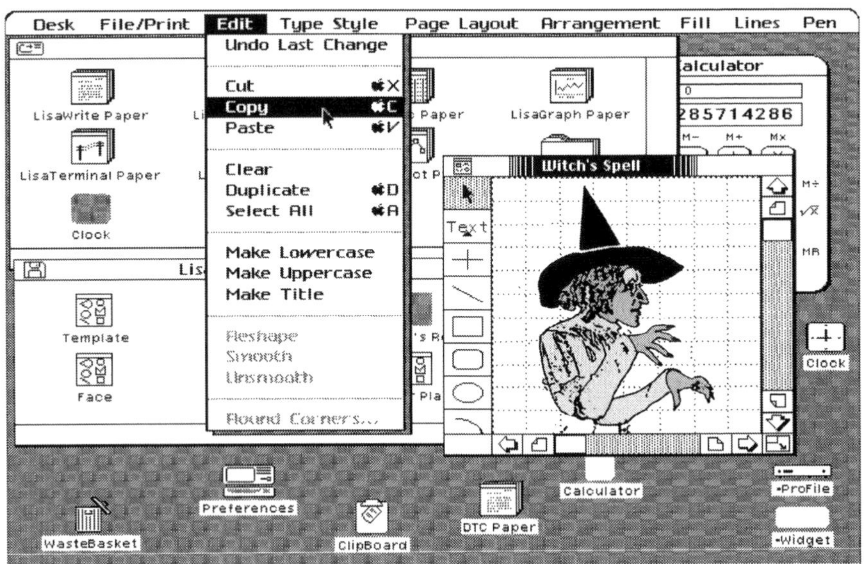

26.

Sometimes you are compelled by force into a decision that you know is for the best but that comes across as completely irrational. I mean, imagine if you had to sit down across the table from someone you didn't know very well and say to them: I've decided to destroy Lisa 2, the computer. It's in everyone's best interest. Putting it like that sounds pretty out there. But let's continue down this line of thinking for a moment and consider methods. Of course, the most practical one is drowning, which I have given a good bit of thought to. After all, the lake is nearby (less creepy than the upstairs bathtub), and I can't imagine anyone dredging it for Lisa 2, unless one of the local law-enforcement officials (I can picture a wet-behind-the-ears rookie taking some sentimental interest in the case just because the computer happens to share a woman's name) decides this is the case that will make his name on the police force and in the community.

But there is something sick about the idea of drowning Lisa 2 and, as satisfying and dramatic as it would be, I decide against it. Putting it in a sack with some rocks and tossing it in the lake just does not feel right. My arm tingles against it. Besides, I would always know it was down there beneath me as I swam, and what if part of it floated to the surface somehow? I can just picture the mouse on the water and Marin screaming.

No, not the lake, not by drowning.

And after all, doesn't Lisa have the right to

create any sort of play she wants, regardless of genre? As far it goes, yes, but the deeper Lisa travels in this new direction the greater the chance it will infect the family itself. It already has done so. I haven't bothered to detail all the small, subtle changes, because the very fact that I have noticed them would probably reflect more poorly on me than on Lisa, to an outsider. Plus, they are such small things—often gestures or turns of phrase or little tics, like how Lisa no longer looks Marin in the eyes when she's talking to her.

The other thing is, why be so drastic and destroy the computer? Even the word destroy probably comes off as a little dramatic. But think about it: I can't very well hide the computer, because that would raise all sorts of questions and might even end up backfiring, and I can see Lisa blaming Marin, somehow, for its disappearance. No, a clean break has to be made. And it's not like I'm going to take a baseball bat to it. My plan is to simply squeeze some glue into the floppy drive slot.

Being open and honest is something I've learned is important, no matter how ugly or uncomfortable the truth is. That, at least, is one lesson I took away from Mom's immolative death: calling it an accident did not change the fact that it wasn't an accident at all. And while I understand why Dad continued to call it that, the one thing I couldn't piece out was, did he believe it? Did he believe his own lie? Everyone knew she killed herself. But I also lied, in a way—a lie of omission. The only person I have ever told about how Mom called my name before setting herself on fire was my therapist. But that was years later, in the neutral comfort of an office, after we sold the hops farm and auctioned off the drying floors that my dad and I had built in the barn. I'll never get the smell of hops out of my head. In fact, I have saved some hops from our very first harvest, in a mason jar.

It is more difficult to get myself alone with Lisa 2 than I had expected. The past few days Lisa has been on a real writing jag and is hardly ever away from the computer. Plus, Marin has been exceptionally clingy lately, something I can ascribe only to Lisa's neglect. Thankfully, we've decided to stay this year into the Cherry Festival, which happens to be a week earlier than usual, and this afternoon Lisa and Marin are taking the winding drive up to Traverse while I stay here and put a fresh coat of paint on the back door. As I stand there and wave goodbye, I can feel the little bottle of glue in my shorts pocket. As soon as the car disappears I head upstairs.

The computer sits there innocently. If anything, it looks inviting, the slimness of the machine and the pleasing way the horizontal floppy-disk slot is mirrored by the thin horizontal grooves in its plastic. The colorful Apple logo stands out, almost like a piece of candy attached to the front with a wad of gum. I approach slowly, as if not to startle the computer, which is silly, but it just feels right In fact, everything is perfect: the slant of light through the window and onto Lisa's papers on the desk, the creak of the wood floor beneath the braided area rug, the gentle whir of the old ceiling fan, the three neat stacks of books on the floor beside the desk. If Lisa and Marin were to return right now, I don't know what I would do. My heart would just break.

I remove the glue tube from my pocket and as squeeze the glue into the slot I realize what an intimate, penetrative thing it is I'm doing. With the tail of my shirt, I wipe away the excess. Then I stand back and admire my work. Not that there's anything to see.

By the time I'm back downstairs the glue should already be doing its work, dripping into the innards of the machine. In the kitchen, I glance at the hidden door in all its malignancy and feel the sudden urge to pull out the mirror-thing inside and smash it to pieces. I don't know why I feel this way, and thankfully the urge passes and I do the wise thing and just ignore it, ignore the hostile door and try to forget what lies behind it.

27.

The question is, how will Lisa react?

As it turns out, she does not react at all, because there is nothing to react *to*. How was I to know that Aunt Elle was loose enough with her money to have extra memory installed in Lisa 2, which back in the mid-'80s must have cost a pretty penny. Was Lisa even *using* floppy disks to save her plays? It does not cross my mind until she comes downstairs late this afternoon with freshly printed pages she said she has just written, obviously not using the floppy drive. Marin is upstairs in her room and Lisa is wearing denim overalls over a pink T-shirt. Her feet are bare. She looks so young.

Hey, good lookin', Lisa says, winking.

I don't think I've ever heard her use that phrase before. It's corny but she doesn't say it in a corny way.

Hey yourself, I say, winking back.

Wanna get married and have a kid? Live on a farm? Create world-changing art but never have to talk to anyone about it?

Whatever it is she's doing, I want to play along.

You mean, I say, someone just shows up, plunks down a monster wad of cash, hauls the art away, and comes back six months later for more?

How about two monster wads of cash?

Even better, I say.

I'm just telling ya, man, I'm on a roll, she says, holding the pages up.

We never talk like this. Lisa never calls me man. I just go with it.

So, your agent, she just waltzes in here, right, quick-checks your pages, plunks down, what, a hundred grand?

I'm just saying there's a potentiality for that.

I recognize that line—or at least the word *potentiality*—from a movie based on an Elmore Leonard novel recommended to me by a defrocked professor, and it makes me wonder if other things Lisa has been saying lately are lifted from movies or books. I follow her into the kitchen, where she puts the pages on the table. There is that late-afternoon softness in the air and it's so quiet I can hear the soft sound of the lake. Then she surprises me, saying she's worried about Marin.

Don't you think she's been acting moody lately, withdrawn? Lisa asks. Do you think it has to do with her ears? Do you think she even knows what's happening, I mean really knows?

Lisa stands at the kitchen window, her back to me, looking out into the yard, into the weird orange light, a *Close Encounters of the Third Kind* light.

I think she's just growing up, I say, taking a seat at the table. I'm tempted to look over at her pages, but I wait, seeing if she will offer them to me. Then Lisa says something that I will never forget: I never wanted her anyway.

The improvident sentenc hangs there, once spoken impossible to be unspoken. She looks me straight in the eyes when she says it, as if to drive the point home. Her voice is flat, affectless; there is no hate in what she says, no anger, no resentment, and somehow that makes it even worse.

This is the true emergence of Lisa 2.

28.

Rewind forty years.

This is what I have to do.

It comes to me in a flash.

I have to do one of my reiterations on Lisa 2, rewriting the short thread of history woven into Aunt Elle's life when she acquires the computer. It's like an on/off switch: in the on setting the past is as it is, and Aunt Elle gets the computer in 1983. In the off setting, Aunt Elle never crosses paths with the computer, hence it never appears here in the cottage, wasn't stored beneath the stairs, hence Lisa never found it. And, having never found it, she can't have entered her new style of playwriting, can't have transformed into someone I no longer recognize as my Lisa.

It actually doesn't come to me in a flash. It comes to me based on a moment from what was probably my favorite class from college, a film class. We watched *Invasion of the Body Snatchers,* the original from the '50s. On VHS on a TV with a tube that would soon blow out. I remember we were asked to focus on how the movie was a commentary on the Cold War, on the paranoia over communism. But that's not what stuck with me as much as the part about falling asleep, because apparently that's when they get you, that's when the aliens snatch your body. *We can't close our eyes all night. We may wake up changed*. There was a scene I have always remembered. The heroes (they seem to be heroes, but are they or have they been taken over?) are bathed in mud. Because the film is in black and white I think of the mud as blood. The film permits me to do this, and so I do. They are bathed in blood.

We may wake up changed.

Lisa has changed, and now I need to change the thing that changed her, the other Lisa. The computer.

I need to change it into something else.

As far as reiterations go, this one is tricky, because I don't have a client *per se*. In a sense, I am my own client, although I like to think I'm working on Marin's behalf, because it's her I want to protect from the newly emerging Lisa. 1983 may seem like a long time ago, but it's more recent than you might think. To do the reiteration I need more than just the computer, though without the computer it's impossible. I need at least some narrative thread about how Aunt Elle acquired Lisa 2. I happen to be in luck because, dedicated preservationist that she was, she kept not only the box the computer came in but all its documentation, including the purchase order from SafeArms, the insurance company she worked for, in a large envelope at the bottom of the box.

I had known the story of how the Lisa 2 was just a pricey warm-up for the Macintosh, but still was surprised to see the amount she paid: $9,500. What did Aunt Elle do with Lisa 2, exactly? There is no evidence of work product, no filing cabinet with printouts. There is, however, one floppy disk, but it seems to be some sort of utility disk. Perhaps there are other parts of Lisa 2 at her insurance company, which just happened to be right next door to Three Scoops, the ice cream shop.

The main thing I need is a set of stable facts: the fact of the computer itself, the fact of its purchase date, and, most difficult of all, the fact of Aunt Elle's first interaction with the computer. But that's just the bare minimum, enough to ensure its erasure from Aunt Elle's life but not enough to make it smooth and seamless, not enough to make the reiteration artful. For that I need not only the facts but a few people (players) to reenact them, to perform Lisa 2's delivery to Aunt Elle and her first experience with it. We'll need to do this little re-creation twice: once with the computer, and a second time without it, just pretending it's there, or else delivering something else in its place, something innocuous. This second time—this second iteration—will replace the first one. There will be no Lisa 2. She—the computer, I mean—will be removed from Aunt Elle's life.

And the players? I am already thinking about that. For Aunt Elle I am going to recruit the librarian who watched as Marin escorted the moth out of the library. For the computer-delivery person, it has got to be Paul, from the ice-cream shop.

It should be simple, because the rewrite involves an object rather than a person. After all, it's just a computer we're talking about here! A piece of machinery, basically, that needs to be removed from Aunt Elle's life, and hence her cottage, and hence Lisa's life. Like I've said before, Lisa 2 was not even designed to be a word processor, as far as I can tell. It was more of a tool to help you organize files, do your budget, keep track of accounts in an easily updatable way. It's just a computer! It was delivered, back in 1983, and it can be undelivered. Nothing is undeliverable! It's just a computer! Just a computer! Lisa, just a computer!

I’m sitting in a sunny café in Marquette, a little college town on the shore of Lake Superior in Michigan’s Upper Peninsula. It’s late August.

If I’m really gone, then how would I know I’m sitting in a sunny café in Marquette, a little college town on the shore of Lake Superior in Michigan’s Upper Peninsula?

When I get to the point in my telling where I disappear, words fail me, and I am sitting in a sunny café in Marquette, a little college town on the shore of Lake Superior in Michigan’s Upper Peninsula, in late August.

I knock at the door, she answers, and I go back to the car.

I deliver the computer and as I approach the station wagon and reach out to touch the car’s door handle, I’m sitting in a sunny café in Marquette, a little college town on the shore of Lake Superior in Michigan’s Upper Peninsula and it’s late August.

My hand brushes Lisa's as I deliver the box to her and I have a chance to stop it but I'm curious about what it would be like to be Lisa, so I play along and go back to the car and I'm sitting in a sunny café in Marquette, a little college town on the shore of Lake Superior in Michigan's Upper Peninsula, in late August.

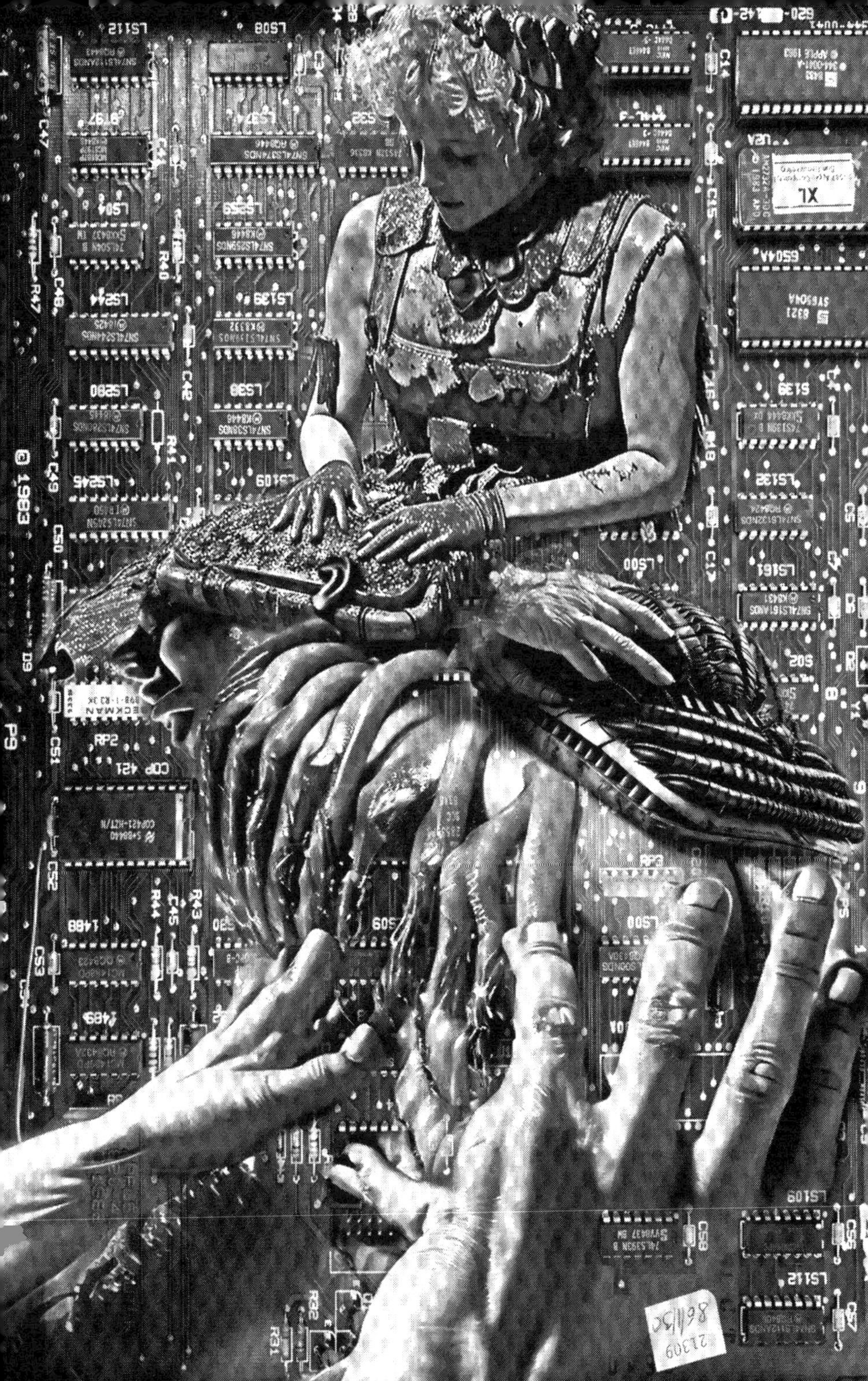

I. Lisa

1.

The first play I ever wrote (well, the first good one) was about a young woman who, in seeking revenge on her cheating husband, purchased an illicit and highly unstable therapeutic to make him forget chunks of his life. As a result, he would have to rely on her (his parents had died years ago and he was an only child) to reconstruct his life story, which was easy for her, since she'd been collecting vintage family photographs from the '70s and '80s—the era of her husband's youth—and had even prepared several shoeboxes full of these photos, carefully selected and curated to create her own version of his so-called life story.

What drew me to this plot as something that could be staged was its clean, direct simplicity. The husband was played by two actors who looked similar but whose mannerisms were slightly different, to represent the intact-memory-husband and the broken-memory-husband. The trick in writing his character was to keeping the audience from empathizing with him too much, especially since I hadn't dramatized his affair or the damage it did to their marriage. I knew that by focusing on the wife's revenge—especially as we witness the husband struggle to regain his memories, which end up being *false* memories—there was a risk that the audience might feel excessive good will for him, disrupting the balance I wanted to achieve between the wife's hurt and the husband's punishment.

I solved this by introducing a third character: their thirteen-year-old daughter. I felt comfortable doing this because we (my husband David and I) did not have Marin yet (she was a few years away), relieving me of the worry that audiences would perceive the play as autobiographical. It was through the daughter that the aftershocks of the affair were depicted, as she sensed the thick tension in the house, so heavy that it forced her deeper into her own imagination. She was played by an actor whose expressive performance while she was painting was like a new art form, something that went beyond acting or dancing. She ended up stealing the show, and when people remember the play they seem to remember her, the daughter, and are fuzzy about the plot itself.

Oh, grow up, will you.

This was the husband's reaction when finally confronted by his wife, who had secretly known about the affair for months, and this also was the mantra their daughter carried around in her head, which poisoned her own happiness. What she saw of the world was always clouded by that phrase—its blame-shifting, its sarcasm, its dismissiveness—and her paintings were expressions of this broken world. This young woman became the central figure in the play, someone who had to come to terms not only with her father's betrayal of her mother but also with her mother's awful revenge. She gave each of her paintings the same title: *Never Grow Up (NGU)*.

The Betrayals ends—when the daughter is a grown woman and a renowned artist—in the aftermath of a fire that ravaged the studio where she paints and where all her artwork is stored. Despite the fact that the studio burns to the ground—all that's left are ashes and a metal doorknob—the paintings are somehow unharmed, and as bloody and vibrant as ever. Within a decade they become cult objects and then religious objects. A shrine is built to house them, and then a church, and then—a hundred years in the future—something like a cathedral, and then many cathedrals. And then *NGU* is the only religion in the world. The final ten minutes of the play are staged in black with no lights.

I say all this because I have come to believe that David's idea for what he came to call the reiterations was rooted, if only obscurely, in this early play of mine. This was at the beginning of our marriage, in the late '80s, a time when I shared my work freely with him. We were living in Chelsea, Michigan, a little village not far from Ann Arbor. Jiffy Mix (well, the company that makes it, Chelsea Milling Company) is located there. It's weird little bohemian town that has the look of a nineteenth-century postcard but the undercurrent vibe of 1968. We lived in a little yellow house overlooking a farmer's field of sunflowers and kept the doors and windows open all summer. We went shoeless, even into town. I wore paisley triangular headscarves (I was in love with Anna Karina) and worked on my plays out in the barn. David loved *The Betrayals* and even wanted to be in it, even though he could not act.

But that was long ago and I bring it up only because it occurs to me, sitting in this sunny café in Marquette, a little college town on the shore of Lake Superior in Michigan's Upper Peninsula, that David was paying closer attention to the plot of that play than I had thought. It's late August, and the students are just starting to trickle back, and in about an hour I will make my way across the Commons—lush from a recent rainstorm—to my office, in the oldest building on campus. I'll print my syllabi, water my plants, clean out and freshen up the mini-fridge, and probably linger to listen to the cicadas singing outside my window, which overlooks the pea-gravel pathway that leads to the small theatre, where one of my plays will be staged this Fall. Along the shoreline, Lake Superior is emerald green in a way that's so astonishing you could imagine you're in the Bahamas. But then—even in late summer—a sudden gust of wind coming in just right over the lake will chill you to your core, no matter how warm the day.

But it's David who is on my brain today, as he is most days, like a pest, nibbling around the edges of my thought. I can't capture his voice, which is funny if you think about it. I had known David for twenty-five years, was married to him for eighteen, and still can't get the rhythm of his speaking down in prose. But in dialog? Well, that's a different story, and I suppose that's why I'm a playwright and not a novelist, because a play is all dialogue, no exposition. And even when characters talk to each other in a novel it can feel, well, novel-ly, you know?

What happened that summer is, in retrospect, either really sad or bitterly absurd. I guess I've finally settled on both. Sad and absurd, as well as some other things: surreal, tragic, even funny, in a slanted way. There is a fearful director I admire, Kiyoshi Kurosawa. Not *that* Kurosawa but the one who's still living, whose films are hard to pin down in the best possible way. They are horror and can be truly terrifying, but they're also sad and unstable, and sometimes they can be absurd in an existentialist sort of way. People who like Kurosawa have their favorites, but mine is *Creepy*, from 2016. I think the full title is *Creepy: False Neighbor*. The creepy neighbor, indeed.

That smile!

The strange thing is, it was only when David began to see me as Lisa 2—a different version of the woman he had married, supposedly because of the computer—that I began to see him as the False Husband. It's as if his suspicions about me somehow boomeranged back on him.

Poor David.

Poor David and his so-called reiterations, which finally devoured him.

My love of him survived all his attempts to scald it out of existence, even when he began calling himself an author. I wish I could say I had seen this coming, this competitive part of David, but I have to be honest and just admit it: I was blindsided. I don't even think it was ego, really, because David was so insecure, so fragile, which is one of the reasons I loved him so deeply, maybe because I recognized—in his vulnerability—my own.

2.

To get to the heart of David's disappearance you have to cross a lot of mental hurdles; at least I did. Marin's another story.

The hardest part was disguising it, my plan, and I think I did this so well that I practically hid it from myself. What I mean is, once I came up with the solution to the problem of David I had to be very careful not to show my hand, this in a family where detecting little signals and seeing beneath the surface was practically an art form. Marin was the worst—or should I say the best—of all, tuned in to the slightest familial undercurrents and disturbances. She knew sometimes before I did when David was getting into one of his moods, as if she could detect something—some dark thought—incubating there inside him before it expressed itself. How she telegraphed this to me is hard to describe. Sometimes it was simply an offhand comment or question, like Is Daddy making breakfast today? (half-signed, half-spoken) when she clearly could see that I was the one starting breakfast. It was little asides like these that alerted me to Marin's own sense that something was wrong, or was soon to be wrong. The strange thing is, it was around the time that she began to lose her hearing that she began to detect that something was off with her dad, as if the partial loss of one sense was balanced by the gaining of another.

When I first began writing plays, the main obstacle was never feelings but rather ideas, plot. I seemed to be a natural at all the other elements: pacing, blocking, voice, characterization, tension, and conflict, both psychological and physical. But for the life of me I was stumped when it came to plot. Story. What to write about? I was cursed with the belief that it had all been done before, better than I could ever do it. In one of my workshops, the professor suggested I dispense with plot and just write what I felt, rather than what I thought I was supposed to feel. This was so simple, yet so freeing.

I'm sure that over time the partners in every long-term relationship develop their own peculiar wrinkles, habits, quirks, and ways of being that may seem odd or eccentric to outsiders, and I think that's what happened with the reiterations. They first appeared in our marriage when Marin was four and David was working as a consultant for the Department of Energy. We lived then in Rockville, Maryland, close enough to D.C. for him to commute, and that's when "Jay" first entered the picture. I remember it well because Marin was running a high fever and, panicked, I tried and couldn't get ahold of David, his cell going right to voicemail and his little-used number at the DOE just ringing and ringing. It was so unlike David, this open-field silence, as if he had fallen out of my world for the hours I needed him most. By the time he returned home, late that night, his cellphone dead because he forgot his charger, Marin's fever had broken. And that's when Jay's name first came up, as a new DOE client David had been assigned to, a man I never met, even though David spent the next two years working closely with him as they developed more efficient catalyst layers for fuel cells, drawing on David's Ph.D. work in materials science.

That's not really what they were developing.

In fact, Jay was not Jay at all, at least not in the conventional sense.

Which is to say, Jay was not even his real name.

3.

Even now, today, with all I know, I still don't know everything. I probably never

will. You would think as a playwright I'd be okay, even happy, with this ambiguity. After all, it was David Mamet's *The Cryptogram*—which is basically ambiguity piled on ambiguity turnstiled into further ambiguities—that got me hooked on writing plays in the first place. But plays are not real life. I don't like unsolved puzzles, or unmade beds, or untended gardens, or unresolved trouble in relationships, or people I cannot clearly read.

I need stable ground.

I need fixed ideas to guide me; otherwise it's all meaningless chaos.

Meaningless chaos is fine in art, but not in real life.

Even if they are pretend, I need fixed ideas.

So, no, I am not at all happy with the fact that I can't pinpoint exactly when David began to believe in the reiterations, or what back then he called "the copies." Remember when I said that David likely got the germ of the idea from my first play, the one about the wife who erases swaths of her husband's memories, only to rebuild them with false ones? The connection, I think, has to do with creation myths, or maybe the better phrase is negative creation myths. Because when you get right down to it, writing a play—or a novel or story, or making a movie or a musical—involves creating a world that doesn't so much replace our sense of lived experience as fit itself over the top of it. In my writing, I like to think that the most important part of the story is also the least visible. No one remembers being born and yet some would say those moments are the most formative of our lives. David must have taken something from this idea—maybe from watching me work on my plays—and imported it into his work, developing the reiterations.

The first time I heard about them was in connection to Jay, whose real name was Jesus, with a hard *J*, hence Jay, whom David had been meeting in the unfinished wing of the DOE building, an area that was never completed because of budgetary cuts. This is where David was during Marin's fever, working on his little machine that would theoretically copy, cut, and replace one small sliver of a prior event with a duplicate, except slightly altered.

It's like gene splicing, he said.

Our shoebox apartment in Rockville was on the sixth floor, and we were out on the little balcony, which gave us a nice view of Town Square. I loved the way sound traveled up; you could make out the voices of the people down below, the occasional peals of laughter from bar-hoppers, the once-in-a-while car alarm. It was a warm autumn twilight and David looked so relaxed in his goofy but charming Hawaiian shirt, the last of the sun falling on him just right. I think I loved him more then than ever before, even as he was crumbling before my eyes.

L: How is it like gene splicing?

D: You cut something out, and put something different in.

L: Is that how gene splicing works?

D: From what I've heard. Obviously, ours isn't that complicated.

L: And what does the DOE think of this?

D: C'mon, Lisa, they don't know!

L: So, what did you cut out, and what did you put in?

D: Two years ago, Jay sat at a booth at Knight's Steakhouse which hadn't been cleared and pocketed the ten-dollar tip that had been left there. He's felt guilty ever since. Last week I went back to Knight's, the same booth, had lunch, left ten bucks on the table. Jay comes in and sits at the booth and doesn't pocket the tenner. That's how he remembers it now. No more guilt.

L: But it's a false memory. That's not what really happened.

D: That's just the point: it *didn't* happen.

That exchange was the beginning of it all, at least for me, for us. Until David actually came out and told me what he was up to I could pretend that what I suspected was going on was just a bit of paranoia on my part. I knew, for instance, that what David said he had been working on at the DOE was not *really* what he was working on, but it was not until the ten-dollar-tip story—which he compared to gene splicing!—that I understood how deep into it and lost he was getting.

4.

There is something sad but also funny that it was my aunt's old vintage Lisa 2 that brought it all to a head for us. For what it's worth, I never used the word notional to describe my horror cycle and I honestly don't know where David came up with that term except maybe from the Eugene Thacker stuff he was always trying to get me to read. He could be such a cosmic doom fanboy. Much of what David remembered and believed is actually true, but the difficult part is that he believed in the things that *aren't* true just as strongly. The whole Zora Neale Hurston "floating line" thing, for instance: I still have no idea how he transformed this small glitch in the photo (a glitch that had always been there) into something sinister. It's true I researched Hurston's anthropological fieldwork for my master's, but the focus was never on voodoo or zombies but rather on the relationship between social class and belief systems in the period following the racist occupation of Haiti by the U.S. Marines beginning in 1915. What fascinated me, luring me into the deep waters of Hurston's thought, was how she never mentioned U.S. imperialism in *Tell My Horse*. And yet, I thought, that is exactly what the book was about! I'm reminded of this when I think of Lisa 2. I sometimes wonder if the computer had been called, say, Meredith 2 or Keith 2, would events have unfolded like they did?

Did it all boil down to the weird luck that we had the same name?

I remember the day David found Lisa 2, tucked away in that little closet space beneath the stairs in the cottage. We set it up first on the farm table in the kitchen, plugged it in, turned it on, saw that eerie gray flow from the screen. Marin was with us and at first thought it was a TV. It was so unlike her tablet, this bulky thing that must have seemed to her like a prop from one of those old science-fiction movies we watched together.

Does it have the internet? Marin asked.

L: No, honey, it's not set up for that.

D: This was made before the internet. People had no idea. Email wasn't even a thing yet.

M: Whose was it?

L: Your aunt Elle's. She used it for keeping track of things at her job.

D: And also to . . .

L: We don't know about that.

What David had wanted to say was that Aunt Elle also used it to write her poems, which she published in a few small journals in the late '80s. I remember this conversation well because it was the day David confronted me about the so-called wolf doodles he had found, and which he attributed to me, although we both knew they were Marin's. We were down by the lake and David was in his ridiculous Speedo and sandals.

D: I don't see how it's good for Marin to see them. They're violent.

L: First of all, drawings can't be violent. And second, of course Marin saw them, because she's the one who drew them.

D: How aren't they violent?

L: They depict violence but they're not violent in and of themselves.

D: I just don't see how it's healthy for her to see your . . .

L: But they're not mine, they're hers.

D: She said you drew them.

L: That's because you scared her, you confronted her with them. What did you expect her to say?

It went back and forth like this, as the lake turned from turquoise to navy and a family in a dented steel canoe waved at us. It was the first time I had seen others on the lake, almost as if our argument had drawn them there. It was actually their presence that interrupted us as they waved and then I waved and somehow that small break took the wind out of our tiff.

And then from out of the blue came the call of a daytime owl we sometimes heard up in that part of Michigan, probably a barred owl with its *hoohoohooHOOaww*.

For a moment I thought it sounded like a wolf.

5.

I have to go back to the unboxing of Lisa 2 and the weird gray light because it really was not like any other light I had seen before. I remember once reading somewhere that we will never really understand the feeling of Victorian-era homes that were lit by gas flames, the reddish orange glow and the flickering. It's a lost experience that we can imagine but never really feel. That's the vibe I got after we turned on the computer, like we were seeing a flow of light unique to these old '80s screens, historical light, unlike the blue light from our laptops and tablets. It felt cold somehow and, as absurd as it sounds, even menacing, as if some little glowing evil were leaking out. I noticed it in the way it shone on Marin's face, as she was short enough to be in front of the screen head-on, and the way it just flowed and pulsed across her forehead and cheeks. Then again, *Poltergeist* came out around the same time as the Lisa 2 so maybe I was just conflating them, but I don't think so. There was something genuinely *not right* about the light and I even told Marin not to stand so close to the screen.

Then suddenly a flash of violent images, like in a waking dream.

Right after I asked Marin to step back came these flickering images of some demented black-and-white avant-garde film: a knife spinning on a wooden table, a cat baring its fangs, a moth crawling out from beneath a girl's eyelid, a flock of blackbirds diving suicidally into a lake. In college I took a film class where we watched a few of Maya Deren's experimental short films from the '40s and I will always remember one scene where she's sitting at a kitchen table (she appeared in her own films) and then another version of herself comes in and sits down, and then another. Three Maya Derens, and then a knife appears on the table, and then its suddenly it's in the palm of her hand, painted black.

Maybe that memory was the source of my perception of the light flowing out of Lisa 2, somehow corrupting Marin, I feared, as if she were receiving secret knowledge that only an adult should know.

It was David's idea that I should try Lisa 2 as a word processor, and to avoid any further discussion I went along with it. We brought it upstairs to my writing space that night, after Marin went to bed. It's funny how the tension between us dissipated as we set up the computer and printer on my desk, then tried to locate the disk with the word-processing software on it. It was as if we slipped back into our old us-against-them vibe from early in our marriage, when solving even the smallest of problems together forged us into a team. Dragging the mattresses up the narrow stairs and into the apartment, figuring out how to keep open the windows that kept slamming shut because their frames were too big, finding the cheapest pizza in town. Somehow, in working through the configurations of Lisa 2, we fell back into our old, happy routine, not even needing to talk with each other as we managed the cords, the power strips, the floppy disks, making sure to position the computer just right on the desk so the bright morning sun wouldn't wash out the screen.

I think this was my last natural, happy moment with David, the David I had fallen in love with all those years ago.

6.

It was Marin who actually used Lisa 2 the most. I used it too, of course, starting but not finishing *Kristy and Marlene* and *Bloodsport*. But it was Marin who was fascinated by the clunky mouse (with a cord!) and the simplicity of the word processor. For some reason, the eerie light emanating from the screen didn't seem so eerie once we moved the computer upstairs, and so I was actually happy to let Marin use it. What did she write? Mostly it was like a diary or a journal, the sorts of things you would expect eight-year-olds to describe: her room, her toys, the songs she liked, her favorite cartoon, the lake. She even mentioned K-pop. I hadn't known she was familiar with K-pop.

But then there was the upside-down tower, and her description of this was so much more detailed and focused than the other things she wrote. In fact, the upside-down tower was almost like a character, a person, and in just a few sentences she described how it came floating over the lake, its windows like eyes, and hovered over the firepit out back, expanding and shrinking rhythmically, as if it were breathing. She actually wrote that: *as if it was breathing*. Her story about the tower was more complicated than her other writing, especially in the way she took the point of view of the tower itself. There was something childlike but also very mature about it all:

> *I've broken from the rest of the church and am now drifting across the lake. I can hear the little ducks beneath me, even though I can't see them. I bet they don't know a tower is floating above them. The cottage is in the distance. That's where I'll find the firepit.*

And then, when the tower arrives at the firepit, the point of view changes, and becomes that of the purple lighter that I had tossed in there. I will never understand why David rooted around in the ashes for this, except that here was just another sign of how he was changing. It was not paranoia, exactly, but close to it, something like an elevated suspicion. But in Marin's story there is none of that, although there is the fact of the lighter, which of course she had seen me toss away as we came up from the beach.

Marin was guileless, open, free in a way that only children can be, showing me what she had written, insisting I sit where she had been sitting as she typed at my desk, in my chair with the extra cushions.

Do you have a title for it yet? I asked.

M: I don't want one.

L: All stories have titles. What would you call this one?

M: What?

L: I said, What will you call it?

Whenever I raised my voice like this I worried she would think I was angry. This was when raising your voice helped. Within two years she would lose her hearing completely.

M: It doesn't have a title because it's not *done* yet.

L: I love the part about the ducks.

M: I just added that. I'm going to give them names.

L: The ducks?

M: It's a family. They each have a name. How do you spell Persifonee?

L: P-E-R-S-E-P-H-O-N-E

M: That's going to be the lady duck's name.

L: Do you know who she was?

M: She was a myth, Mommy. We learned about it.

That's how we talked about her story. It struck me that learning about ancient Greek and Roman myths was the first step in deconstructing our own myths, not that we call them myths. The Greeks understood and made sense of the changes in the seasons through Persephone, queen of the underworld, having been kidnapped by Hades. Marin was learning about the Persephone myth, but was she also learning about how—because our sense-making stories of the world change over time—it means that none of them, in the end, are "true"? Or maybe the average ancient Greek did not really believe the Persephone story anyway? Or, maybe they believed it and didn't believe it at the same time, sort of half-believed it, just as Persephone spent half her time in the underworld with Hades and the other half with her mother Demeter above the world, on Mount Olympus?

As we chatted about Persephone and the upside-down tower, I noticed how Marin was holding the Lisa 2 mouse, cradling it almost. She might even have petted it as it rested there in the palm of her hand. It was sort of a boxy thing, not sleek and oval like the later versions. She took one of the plastic Minnie Mouse barrettes from her hair and placed it on the desk and then put the mouse beside it.

Two mice, she said.

Then David came in.

Then everything changed.

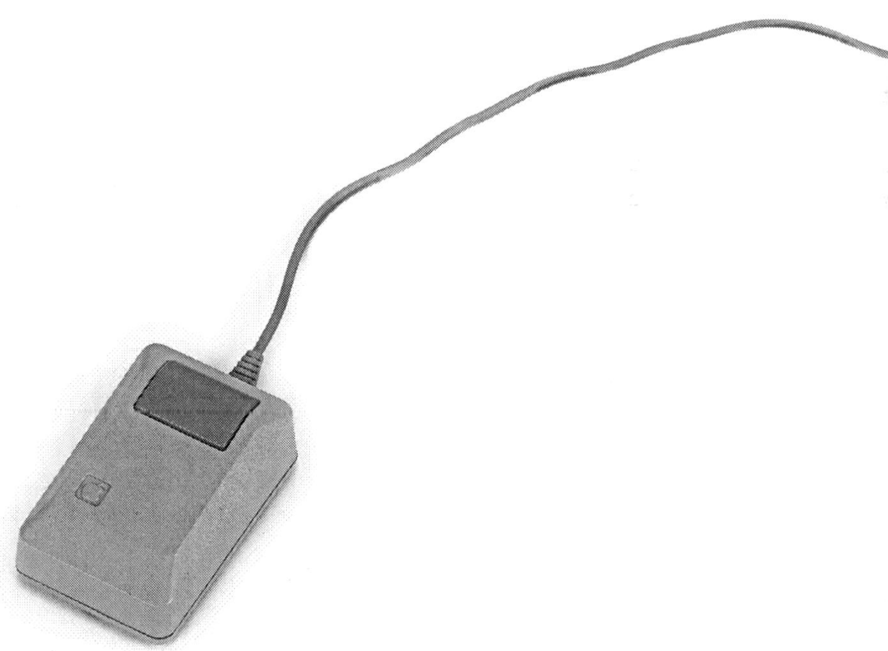

7.

I have to say—or maybe confess?—that the more David devolved, the more I loved him, despite the fact that his changing was clearly the beginning of the end for us. What I mean by loving him more is that it was like I was falling in love with a new person, an extension of David that was opening up new parts of him that I had never seen or experienced before. Can I just say for the record that he became a better kisser? I don't know how it is with you, but passionate kissing is one of the first things to go in a long marriage. When it came to lovemaking—okay, when it came to fucking—we just cut right to it. How do you seduce someone you have been married to for a while?

But I began to love him for more than just his extended kissing. He had taken to wearing a bandanna (this reminded me a bit of David Foster Wallace, but I don't think David knew who he was), which was sort of cute. He also started to pay more attention to me, even if that attention wasn't always positively focused. What I mean is that he began showing more interest in my writing, even though his motives were born out of suspicion and paranoia. Is it ego to confess that anytime people ask you about what you're creating it's flattering? Even critical, negative attention can be a rush because it means that what you're making matters somehow. So, when David began probing around the edge of my writing, it felt fresh and new, as if I were seeing for the first time a curiosity in him that had been hidden. When it came to our work

I think we kept things fairly practical, and it's true that I had always stressed how writing plays, even though it was "creative," was really just about the work, the labor, the craft. We rarely used words like inspiration, talent, or genius, or any language that suggested something mystical about creativity.

I remember when it first happened, because it was so dramatic.

I think it was the day Marin encountered the moth in the library, and, as I look back on it, maybe it was no coincidence. Her hearing was really going fast around this time, especially in her left ear, so she would often turn her head to the right a little bit when we were talking, as if her left ear were an antenna. Her other antenna was less visible but even more powerful, detecting the subtle shifts in David's moods before they surfaced. A sort of mood sonar.

The first time I remember it happening was at the beginning of that summer, the Lisa 2 summer, as Marin and I were trying to catch butterflies, her new obsession. She was wearing her other new obsession, a dress from her aunt Fernie that she loved so much she would sleep in it if she could, and one night she actually did. We were out in the meadow behind the greenhouse when she stopped in her tracks and said: Daddy. She bolted up to the cottage and by the time I got there she was in David's arms, whimpering, holding him tight.

It's okay, David was saying, stroking her hair. Everything's okay.

She could not even put into words what had happened and it was only years later, when she first started writing and publishing her poetry, that she began to express how this felt, this *electrical thinking* as she phrased it in one of her teenage poems. Later that evening, David came up into my writing space with a glass jar. I heard him coming, or rather I heard what he had in the jar: a cicada. The droning *zwher, zwher, zwher* sound, except muted. He had found the cicada on the screen door and put it in the jar with some grass and twigs and had poked little air holes in the metal lid, just like I did as a girl catching fireflies. Moths, cicadas, fireflies—suddenly my world seemed insectoid.

I know you like being down by the lake, so I thought I'd bring some of the lake up to you, he said, offering me the jar.

Although what he was saying didn't really make sense, I think I understood what he was getting at: he was bringing a bit of the natural world inside. Why? Because he knew it soothed and inspired me, and I have to say this was the very first gesture of its kind in our marriage. It was a bit creepy, sure, but also sweet, that he would bring this singing insect up to me because he knew it would make me happy. There was a part of me that wanted to be loved by David so completely, even as I knew that that kind of total love would destroy me. Did I want to be destroyed? I think a part of me did. A part of me wanted to be smothered by David's love because what he was showing me now was something I had felt only briefly at the beginning of our marriage, when I really did want to abandon myself to his desires, which were also my desires.

And there is the rub, because when you are in love like that there is no separation, no

Venn diagram where intersecting circles meet to indicate shared love. No, instead, the sort of love I'm talking about is all intersecting, all overlapping; the circles are on top of each other, infinite in depth, making it impossible to tease out who loves whom more. Maybe that was our problem, that we had become too connected too early in our relationship, our circles meshing with each other so completely that it became difficult to separate ourselves from each other until that summer at the cottage, when something happened that triggered a long-overdue pulling away from each other, a separation, as if David changed to water and I to oil.

And yet, I began to love him more. The further we separated over that summer the closer I felt to him, the more I wanted him, as if the separation finally allowed me to see his illness fully. Not just to see, as a witness, but to experience. I felt his sickness, the way he felt his sickness, as colonizing, totalizing, complete.

And the Lisa 2 fiasco?

I have to be honest: I completely misread it as a cry for help.

I should have read it as a warning.

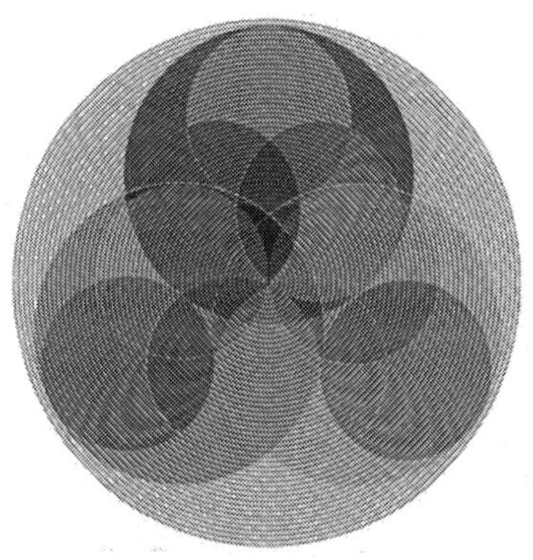

8.

Was it Marin's blossoming creative side that set in motion the events of that terrible summer? After all, the first time I saw *that look* on David's face—the wide eyes and crooked smile—was when he opened the door upstairs and interrupted Marin's upside-down-tower story.

"Two mice . . ." and then, *boom!*, in walks David, all shoulders and neck and flannel shirt and that crazed smile on his lips. It was as if the confluence of the Lisa 2 computer, me, Marin, and her little fantasy story exploded some tiny part of David's brain. I understand now what he must have been thinking: that Lisa 2 had infected not just my writing, but Marin's as well. And the fact that she had typed it up there on the recently discovered computer—it was really the first time she had used a word processor rather than write longhand—must have only cemented his crazy idea that Lisa 2 was somehow guiding not only mc, but now Marin as well, down dark creative pathways.

"Two mice how, sweetie?" David asked, having just entered the room, as if the spigot had been turned from hot to cold. It was the first time I had seen Marin react to her father with anything other than pure joy. Her eyes darted over to mine, as if asking if it was okay to answer his question, and to be honest it, broke my heart a bit, to witness this first chink in the bond between Marin and her dad. She did not need my permission to answer him, and she knew this. On impulse, she handed him the Minnie Mouse barrette as if it were some sort of weird peace offering. Or not even that, really, more like an exchange, or bribe, like she was thinking Here, Dad, take this and in exchange don't ask any more questions. Looking back on it, I think her reaction had more to do with me than with David. What I mean is, this was the first of several instances when Marin started to cautiously reposition herself into my orbit, while pulling herself out of David's. I may never have any way of knowing how much of this was due to the evolving psychology of an eight-year-old coming into her own and how much was due to the disruptive presence of Lisa 2.

But for David, it had everything to do with Lisa 2. In fact, the moment after Marin's eyes shifted to mine, David's shifted to the computer. I could practically read his thoughts, destructive, bright-white thoughts aimed right at the screen. The color even rose in his cheeks and who knows what he would have done had it not been for Marin rising up and running over to him with a page of her story.

I wrote it for you, Daddy, she said.

A feeling of lightness came over me and I understood with clarity that a new being had entered into our tight little tricornered family, and it was already creating space for itself.

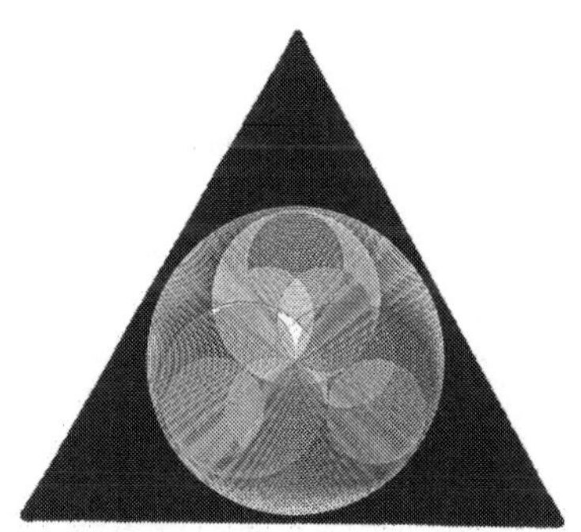

9.

In my plays I have complete control, the freedom to iron out any wrinkles, eliminate the ambiguities, even if only for myself. Audiences love the open spaces in my work, which give them enough room to interpret and debate my endings, but I always know the answers. In *Pieces of Eight*, for instance, I know that Julianne's affair was motivated not by love but by revenge, even if the audience doesn't know this. Or in *All / Hands / On / Deck*, where it's perfectly clear to me that the girl stowaway on the whaling ship survives—is the *only* survivor—of the six-day ice storm in the North Atlantic. Or in *The Delacourt Family Album*, where the relationship between siblings Damien and Theresa is hardly incestuous at all, despite what the Polaroids from the hidden family photo album seem to suggest. Even though these meanings are clear to me, as the playwright, it really does not matter, because once the play is performed live it actually *does* become alive. It awakens from its slumber and becomes this real electrical force with a life of its own.

That's what happened with David's chunk of tree bark with the initials K + M he supposedly received in a package one afternoon at the cottage. I say *supposedly* because, although I saw the bark, I am not convinced it arrived as David said it did. In any case its meaning remains a mystery to me, gnawing at my brain like some slow disease. I have my theories of course, but that's all they are, theories. I suspect that David himself carved the letters and concocted the ruse, but for the life of me I have no idea why. This bothers me and then I feel ashamed for letting it bother me.

After all, what does it matter compared to everything else that happened? And yet, I can't let it go, so sometimes lying in bed at night I will imagine it as a short scene in a play. I can picture the David in the play sitting at the farm table. He wears hiking pants. He practically looks like an REI model. Once I have that visual, everything else falls into place. David's carving the piece of pine-tree bark for Marin to use as a prop in tea parties with her dolls. She is going to pretend it's a little coat of arms; the K + M initials stand for some deep lineage.

Although this is all in my head, it feels real as I lie there at night, the sounds of Lake Superior coming up through my window. This piece of bark makes no sense except when I insert it into an imagined play where I can do with it what I want, assigning it my own meaning, making it conform to my own desire of sense-making. There's an implied violence in this imaginative act, I know.

But then there is a certain violence to any storytelling, isn't there?

Critics talk about art being creative but I know better.

For art to work, it first has to destroy.

Speaking of destruction, it's just like David to think I couldn't sense the guilt he felt about his mother's suicide, if it *was* a suicide. I say *if* because when you look back at the newspaper articles from the time (the story was a big deal for a while because of the nature of Rose's death and the fact that it happened in such a small, rural community), there is ambiguity surrounding her death. Only months later, after the story moved to the back pages, did the official version indicate suicide by self-immolation, apparently such a rare occurrence among American women that there is almost no precedent. I think that's why it took so long to rule this as her cause of death.

The more obvious explanation is that someone else set the barn on fire.

10.

And the absurdity of this "Paul" person David was obsessed with that summer, medieval! I can laugh about it now but at the time I was worried about how David's exaggerated descriptions of the ice-cream shop man might affect Marin. I had actually seen this Paul-worker myself and although it's true he was a large man, there was nothing menacing or monstrous about him. In fact, I was struck by the gentleness of his manner and movements as he scooped out black raspberry and handed me the cone, as if he were passing some precious object across the counter of the ice cream parlor. The way David characterized him was so out of proportion to my understanding of the man that I couldn't help but wonder what Marin must have thought as he conjured a large-handed, melty-faced ogre.

It was then that I saw how, in her effort to please her father, Marin went along with his exaggerations, nodding as David went on and on about the leather apron, the thick black eyebrows, the threatening current he said Paul exuded. Was Marin so susceptible to David's imaginings that she might actually come to believe in this version of the ice-cream man? This wasn't the tipping point in my decision, but there is no doubt it contributed to my understanding that David's world was not suited for Marin, that it even constituted a threat. Her love was so unconditional during those preteen years that even if David had described Paul as a three-headed giraffe she would have nodded and said, Yep, that's Paul all right.

Only years later would I come to see that Marin's tendency to fall into the stories of others had less to do with Paul's exaggerations than with her own budding talent as a writer. Had I known this back then—had I understood that David's stories posed no danger at all to Marin—would I still have taken the path I did, the path that led to David's removal? Would I still have gone through with the plan, a plan that worked better than I could have imagined? I'm probably not the right person to answer that, given that I'm telling my own version of my own story here, but I really do believe that Marin was (and is) better off without David in her life. The force of David's vision—especially during that fateful summer involving Lisa 2—became sort of like a pot of tea that never quit darkening.

I had to stop the steeping.

It's a cliché to blame our parents for everything, but what about our kids, who blames them? No one. No one blames the kids for their misfortunes these days; good parents just don't do that sort of thing. Ours is the age of deflected responsibility, as long as that deflection is targeted at our elders rather than at our offspring. It's Freud's fault. It's social media's fault. It's the Founding Fathers' fault. It's always the older generation, those already dead or dying or soon to be dying. But what if it's our kids' fault? Once I saw Marin's talent—once it became clear that she would be an artist of some sort—I began to resist the gravity of who she was, of who she was becoming. It wasn't that I was in competition with her or that I was jealous—her upside-down- tower thing was nothing to write home about—but rather that I didn't want her to get to where she was headed too fast. I needed my own breathing space, my own center stage, so to speak, without having to look over my shoulder at Marin.

11.

I don't know if David ever really understood how much I disliked it when he called me his Hemingway girl, or his Murakami girl. But then how could he have known, given that I never told him, at least not outright? How many times, after a new hair color or a new cut, would he say something like that, as if I liked either of those authors, let alone their scrawny female characters? Maybe I played along because I knew it made him happy, but I don't think so. It's more complicated. My theory now is that it had something to do with compensation; to compensate for the ways in which I wasn't pleasing David, I gave him permission to call me his Murakami girl.

I remember when it first happened, before Marin came along, and how I stopped myself from saying Don't call me that! We'd just moved into our second apartment, the one with the balcony that overlooked the brook, and David had been reading one of Murakami's novels, *Sputnik Sweetheart,* I think, and instead of stopping him I let him go on, even as he fondled my earlobe, saying something like I can see them now. But I'd just begun a residency at the local arts center and I was gone a lot so I just let him say it—my Murakami girl—happy it made him happy and also happy it might buy me some goodwill regarding my upcoming absence from his life.

It did not work out that way, of course, and it was ridiculous that I resented David for his haircut comments when I could have easily put an end to it. The truth is, I came to use the haircuts as a sort of bait, luring David into his realm of erotic fantasies. In the days after one of these haircuts, David's sense of me became clouded, obscured. The haircuts were distractions that made him overlook how my work didn't conform to his expectations. I found myself getting haircuts just to throw David off my creative trail; at least for a while it gave me space to take a stab at more horror-tinged work.

And now that Marin is coming into her own as a poet, it has become clear to me that pretending to like it when David made me into one of his Murakami girls actually helped me become a more confident writer. I got to feel what it was like to be a character, a construct, from the *inside*. Acting like I didn't mind the way David objectified me into some other type of woman—some fantasy he had based on a young woman in *The Wind-Up Bird Chronicle* or whatever—became a sort of exercise, a performance that I channeled into the *Kristine and Marlene* play I was drafting that summer, on Lisa 2. Pretending to be someone else was what I expected from the actors in my plays, so it seemed only right that I get a taste of it, performing for my own audience of one: David.

Although it's true there was a horror dimension to *Kristine and Marlene*—there's a shocking scene straight out of *American Psycho*—it still remains a mystery to me why he associated the beginning of this horror phase with Lisa 2 when in fact it began much earlier, in works like *The Sarah Syndrome* and *Blank Star*. It's as if Lisa 2 somehow revealed what was already hinted at in my work, like a litmus test. In this sense, David may have been right about the old computer. Maybe there *was* something about it that changed things, just not in the way he thought.

I remember one of our exchanges on the way back from the lake. Marin was trailing behind us, singing to herself, and we were hyperaware of her presence because she had gone missing for a few hours the previous day, having wandered so far into the woods that she couldn't hear us calling. Glancing back at Marin, he said, sort of offhand, something along the lines of *If she goes missing again we should let her stay lost for a little longer*. How could David have known that this was the exact thing I had been thinking for weeks now, not regarding Marin but relating to a new idea for a play I was turning over and testing in my head, a play that would involve parents who justify the neglect of their daughter because they believe it will better prepare her for the cruelties of the adult world?

When David suggested this about Marin—that we should *let her stay lost*—I had to catch myself. How could he have known this was the very drama I was working out, considering I had never spoken about it to anyone? Was it a complete fluke? Or was there something else at work, something we could neither see nor sense? Years later, I've come to believe that this was all connected somehow to Lisa 2, that its presence activated something, some extra sense in David, not in a mystical or supernatural way, but in a way I still don't have the right words for. Come to think of it, it might have been that very afternoon when the thought first crossed my mind about what to do about David.

Or, should I say, *how* to do to David what needed to be done.

12.

I need to say something about the little door in the cottage kitchen and what was behind it, which threw David for such a loop. When I was a girl spending summers there I knew the space behind the door was the place where Aunt Elle kept her cleaning supplies. This must have been right after Uncle Norm died because all his shoe-polish stuff was in there too. Sometimes I would open the door just for the mixed smells of Murphy Oil, Pledge, the shoe-polish tins on the floor. I even hid in there one time, curled up behind the mop bucket as Aunt Elle busied herself cleaning the kitchen, no doubt pretending she didn't know I was in there. So it was never a "hidden" door to me and I'm not sure what drew David to it or why he assigned such malevolence to the old mirror Aunt Elle had stored in there. David's paranoia must have been running high at this point and maybe he was just searching for some sort of confirmation that something was off, in the cottage. Or maybe he thought Lisa 2 was just the tip of the iceberg, that there were other objects in the cottage that would "change" things in the way that the computer was supposedly changing me.

The strange thing—and I could never have admitted this to David—is that I was the one who wrote the DO NOT REVERSE message on a scrap of paper torn from a grocery bag, as part of a scavenger hunt, the summer I was twelve or thirteen. That summer holds a special place in my memory because it was the one when my cousins visited and the scavenger hunt was their idea. Melissa and Rhonda, a few years older than me, were the cousins I did not see often because of some obscure family estrangement. I remember them as sort of hippie-like or countercultural, bohemian, I didn't yet have the word for it. They were super tan with unshaved armpits and seemed free-flowing in their halter tops and denim cutoffs and wild blue and yellow sparkly eyeshadow.

Like girls in the movies, I thought. I distinctly remember lying there in my sleeping bag one night (we slept in sleeping bags on the back porch when they visited) and imagining they were girls from a Dirty Harry movie. I don't even know if there are girls like that in Dirty Harry movies but that's what I thought at the time. It was intimidating having them—especially Rhonda, who was so full of sex—snoring there next to me, having probably slept with Clint Eastwood and maybe the rest of crew, which I imagined was all male, the sort of guys who'd snicker *punk this* and *dirty rotten punk that* between takes.

For the scavenger hunt I hid several notes with instructions like: *Go back to the first room, stop, and turn around and look at the ceiling*, and DO NOT REVERSE.

When David found the note more than twenty years later, I remembered right away; the memories of that summer with my cousins came flooding back. So why didn't I say something, why didn't I tell David where the note had come from and what it meant? Why did I let him torment himself with fantasies of cryptic meanings? I had a writing mentor who once said that when it comes to drama, we don't need to look any further than our own families for material, but I cannot imagine that I could have ever have been so selfish and ambitious as to allow him to flounder with the note's significance just so I could get some material for one of my future plays.

David's recollection about that day can't be right. At least the part about how Marin and I came in from outside with the wildflowers we'd picked, as he was looking at the hidden door in the kitchen. Marin was just beginning to come to terms with her hearing loss and a pall had fallen over her. She was glum. As I remember, she threw the bunch of flowers onto the kitchen floor, and even stomped on them with her rain boots. She blurted out No more flowers! Marin was not the one who asked for a vase, I was, to signal to David that these flowers were important to me and were meant to be preserved. This is important because it's a memory Marin and would laugh about years later, an example of how stubborn she was, and No more flowers! was our catchphrase. I would use it sometimes to make her laugh when she'd get frustrated at something—like how her landlord treated her one time grunting at her, she said. She would be upset and I'd say, No more flowers! and that would usually pull her out of her funk and put a smile on her face.

It still does.

13.

The funny thing is I had known about the computer and understood why Aunt Elle had packed it away beneath the stairs near the back of the little closet. I too had felt its weird, gravitational presence. But, of course, I was its namesake, and so who's to say how that colored my feelings about it? When Aunt Elle said she wanted to introduce me to "another Lisa," how was I to know this wasn't another woman, but a computer? I was seventeen then, a half-dozen years away from marrying David. My aunt had taken to wearing extravagant outfits, at least to my eyes, clothes she bought on her visits to New York City at a secondhand shop that sold costumes from past Broadway shows. She had always been what my mother had called "bohemian" but in later years, after her husband's death, she took it even further, living as if she had nothing to lose. The computer was, I thought, her latest folly, much like the unused greenhouse had been, or the hand-made wooden canoe from Canada she never once put in the lake, or the clay kiln she had built behind the cottage for a pottery hobby that never materialized.

But Lisa 2 was different, an object that for several years sat on the very kitchen table that

David described so well. It existed—unused, as far as I could tell—in the cottage like some museum piece, gathering significance, but of what sort I didn't understand. Oh, I felt its analog presence, even though it was a digital creature. In the years before Aunt Elle's death, as I helped her sell and donate her furniture, art, and jewelry, Lisa 2 remained there on the table. As far as I recall, Aunt Elle never plugged it in, or *hooked it up*, as she'd say, and I remember wondering why, then, it was warm to the touch, as if it had been running.

I told myself that Lisa 2 must have been warm because the sun had been shining on it, through the kitchen window. This was just before the infamous Orwellian (anti-Orwellian?) Super Bowl ad for the Macintosh, which I'm sure I didn't see when it first aired (in 1984!) but later, on one of MTV's news segments, probably with Nina Blackwood. (And oh how I remember wearing out my ears with "Girls Just Want to Have Fun" that summer.) But even before that ad there was an aura around the Lisa computers and even the name Apple. Even then, Apples felt so different than the mpersonal IBMs, which were still associated with the malevolent HAL than*2001: A Space Odyssey*, and maybe that's why Aunt Elle had Lisa 2 so prominently displayed there on the farm table, as a sign that she was forward-looking, young at heart.

In any case, it was only during the last summer I visited, the year before she died, that Aunt Elle put it back in its box and asked me to help her store it in the closet, where it stayed until David found it all these years later. I have this distinct memory of Lisa 2 changing as I lifted it off the table. What I mean—and you have to understand that this was a bulky, heavy computer—is that it seemed to shift weight as I held it, going from heavy to light, as if made of cardboard. Granted I was tired from helping Aunt Elle pack up as well as from the emotional toll of it all—she was distressed and afraid of what the future held for her. But beneath this rationalization, right below the surface, is the other explanation—that Lisa 2 shifted its (her?) own weight somehow, as if . . . as if what?

In retrospect, it all unraveled so fast. Now that Marin's older—and a writer herself—it's her telling of the story that guides my own. But before I get to that, I should say more about David's reiterations, the idea being, as you've heard, that he would re-enact some original event, removing or adding some small detail.

You know the drill, at least David's version.

The original would be replaced.

The copy would become the original.

But what if that's not exactly what happened?

It's a question I have lived with for fifteen years, ever since that last day at the cottage. It was one of those bright, still late-summer mornings; the only sound was the wind in the pines. There's a certain clarity in that kind of unfiltered light, almost a flashbulb sharpness that gives a weird sense of permanence to everything, making it impossible to imagine that any of this would decay: us there in the cottage, the farm table, the daisy-yellow teapot on the stove, Aunt Elle's mushroom-shaped salt and pepper shakers. Marin and I had baked a loaf of apple cinnamon bread and it was cooling on the counter when David came in with the costumes and props.

I was to play Aunt Elle while he was to be the courier for SafeArms, delivering what was supposed to be Lisa 2, except that it wasn't Lisa 2 but rather something else, a twelve-inch TV which—according to the logic of the reiterations—would replace Lisa 2 so that there never was and never had been a Lisa 2 in the cottage that David never would have found and which I would never have used and so my plays never would have changed and neither would I, or so David hoped. If the reiteration worked as planned, the only thing David would have discovered in the closet beneath the stairs would have been the small television. Lisa 2 and everything associated with it would have never existed.

But the fact that I'm writing about it now means it didn't work. Something went wrong. Lisa 2 was not erased from history and replaced by a harmless television. But the reiterations always take something, even if, on rare occasions such as this, it's the wrong thing, or, in this unfortunate case, person.

14.

It's early September and I'm back at the café at my favorite table in Marquette. It's easy for me to write here because the distractions are of just the right sort, allowing me to fall into the world of the play I'm working on without going in over my head. The sound of ceramic on ceramic is soothing and the afternoon sun is coming in through the red glass art on the windows and the place shimmers in a comforting but hellish way. I love this early part of the semester, the gentle dance between students and professors as they get to know each other, before any of their work is graded. I wish the entire semester could be like this, just exploring ideas and art and performance and writing without any consequences, free from hierarchy and judgment. But I know the world doesn't work that way. It's just a fantasy.

The students (well, their parents) are paying good money for them to be taught and evaluated and deemed worthy and I, too, am being paid to judge them, no matter how open and free my classes feel. There is a group of students at the counter in their uniform white sneakers and I recognize one—Lillian?—from my Fundamentals of Screenplay Writing class last semester but neither of us says anything. I'm wearing an oval blue topaz ring (not real!) Marin bought me for my birthday years ago. If I hold my hand just right in the spot of sun on the table it reflects a small circle on Lillian's back, like a target. I adjust my finger and the reflection crawls up the back of her head.

I've promised myself so many times that I'd tell Marin what happened to her father. Fifteen years is a long time for someone to be absent and I can't even say for sure that Marin believes he simply walked away that day, leaving us behind like some coward. In the weeks and then months and then years after the botched reiteration—as Marin turned nine and then ten and eleven—the stories I told her evolved. Her dad had gone on a long assignment for work; he had suddenly been called overseas one night and said goodbye to her while she was asleep; we had separated for a while and he moved in with his brother in Colorado and was too ashamed to contact her. By the time she was in her teens, the story had finally settled on some remote cabin near Ironwood in the Upper Peninsula, where he disappeared to, a place so far west in Michigan that if you drove due south for about a thousand miles you would end up in Arkansas.

I can't say the extent to which she believed any of this but there was enough there—enough wanting to believe—that she never questioned me about it. Maybe she searched for him online; it's possible. If she did, she never asked me about him. It's as if our lives filled the void that David's sudden and permanent absence created, a seam so delicate that neither of us dared to examine it too closely. I think there must also have been a deep sense of guilt, for as much as Marin loved her father she also saw how sad he made me, how disruptive his presence had become in those last years. He was a lot of noise, David was, if that makes sense. He needed caretaking in a way that I couldn't, or wouldn't, provide, and Marin must have sensed that my unhappiness was making us all unhappy. In fact, the week before the blown reiteration, she'd asked about her best friend's parents, who'd moved into separate homes, her friend living with her dad, and her friend's brother living with his mom. I think what she was getting at, but didn't want to come right out with, was how things would work out, living-situation-wise, if David and I moved into separate homes. She was very practical at that age, and I think she must have been working out in her mind where she'd sleep, who would make her breakfast in the morning, who would take her shopping at the mall.

In any case, it somehow came to be that for each month and then year that passed with no David, the stories about what had happened mutated. Of course, I knew what had happened right away, having heard David talk about botched reiterations in the past, either because the re-creation was not as close to the original as it needed to be, or because someone flubbed an important line or gesture, or because of other, more obscure reasons that neither David nor his collaborators ever fully understood.

And yet, on that warm August morning, everything appeared to be in order.

I had found an outfit circa early '80s from the vintage-resale shop in town and David had the TV, which he'd packaged into the original Lisa 2 box. Although you wouldn't think it, with a reiteration like this, from the deeper past, precise details did not matter as much, as if the process somehow knows and adjusts itself to the level of difficulty. David wasn't too worried about having the exact time of day right. And even the things that could corrupt a reiteration of a more recent event, liked missed timings or incorrect gestures and responses, weren't really at play here.

We made sure Marin was in her room. There was no reason to try to hide the reiteration from her—she knew what David did for a living, after all—so we told her, in case she watched from her upstairs window, that there would be a station wagon pulling into the drive (David paid the used-car dealer to borrow it for the day) and that David, dressed in a bland corporate jacket and slacks, would come to the door with a large box, ring the bell, and that I, as Aunt Elle, would answer the door and take the box.

It was more than a little strange, I can tell you, pretending to be puttering around the kitchen dressed as Aunt Elle, waiting for the delivery of what was supposed to be Lisa 2. I could not help but feel I was somehow connecting with my aunt in a way I never had before. She was a recent widow in 1983, my uncle having died from a heart attack in the greenhouse the year before. Was the new computer a diversion, a way to detour her grief into some new thing? I adjusted my wig—Aunt Elle was a redhead all her life—and took the dishes from the strainer and put them in the cupboard while I waited for David, aka the deliveryman.

15.

For the longest time after pulling up in the brown station wagon, David did not get out. It was as if he was having second thoughts. I could imagine him balancing his desire to remove Lisa 2 from existence on the one hand and his concern, on the other hand, that the reiteration might result in some unforeseen wrinkle, some consequence no amount of planning could prepare for or prevent.

16.

Because what David could not know was that what was going to disappear in the reiteration was not Lisa 2 but David himself.

17.

What I'm going to describe may sound cruel, but you have to understand that my love for Marin was different and perhaps more deep than my love for David, so what I did was for her. The idea for sabotaging the reiteration came from David, actually, back in the Maryland days at the Department of Energy when he and Jay were first working out the process. He'd shared that they were worried about a mole, a woman on their team whom they suspected of working for the other side because of how she'd botched one of the early copies (he still called them that back then) by removing (accidentally, she claimed) an item crucial for the process to work. In the resulting copy of the event—the one that now overlaid and replaced the original event—the item was indeed missing, as if it had never existed. It was a simple pink stapler, gone forever.

I had always remembered this story, and how David and Jay worried about how easy it would be to do something like this at a larger scale with an object far more important than a pink stapler. For obvious reasons I can't reveal how I rigged the Lisa 2 reiteration to remove David, but I can say that it worked. Not at first, not immediately, which I still don't understand. The process went as planned: Marin was in her upstairs room, I was waiting in the kitchen as Aunt Elle, David pulled into the driveway in the rented station wagon with the Lisa 2 box that contained the TV, he knocked on the door, I answered, [redacted]

, and he drove away and never came back. I remember standing there with the box in my hand, the sun glinting off the distant lake in little shards of bright yellow light. I remember the way David's hand brushed mine as he handed me the box, thinking how handsome he looked at that moment, and how happy. For a moment I wanted to stop it right then, to just take him by the hand and run into the woods and then keep running.

As I watched him drive off, Marin came down and asked if she could try on the chunky plastic necklace I was wearing as part of my Aunt Elle costume. I gave it to her before going upstairs to change back into my own clothes and as I passed by the upstairs room where Lisa 2 had been I could see the reiteration had worked, at least in part. The computer was still there, on the desk, having not been replaced with the TV. I took off the wig, washed the makeup off my face and, before descending the stairs to rejoin Marin, paused at the landing to listen to her as she talked to herself, playing dress-up with Aunt Elle's necklace. I listened carefully, with eyes shut, letting Marin's voice, from the kitchen, sink into my brain, and I wondered if this would be one of her last moments free from the question of what had happened to her disappeared father.

18.

It's late September now, and most of what I've written I've written here in the café.

Lake Superior is churning now, as it always does in the fall, and you can hear the sound all the way up here by the campus. My classes are going well and my new play, *Alice Doesn't*, opens next Friday at the little theatre on campus. Marin is coming in from Cleveland for the premiere and to read one of her poems at an open mic hosted by the English department. Plus, it's her twenty-fourth birthday on Saturday. She now knows what happened to David, for the most part, although I'm not sure she believes it. Although we live in a world where so many counterintuitive things that should be impossible are real—quantum computing!—it's still hard for her to get her head around the bald fact of the reiterations. Her father's been gone long enough from her life that any attachment she has to him must feel abstract, symbolic. Does she remember how she used to rush up to him like the wind, shouting *Daddy!*, without an ounce of reserve or self-consciousness? Does she remember the elaborate breakfasts he made her on Saturday mornings, or the continuing bedtime story he told her about the bottomless hole in the field behind the farmer's barn?

I say that Marin *mostly* knows what happened to David, because there are details I haven't shared with her, and why should I? What good would it do her to know that I'd tampered with the Mead-Fancher machine just enough so that

David would never come back? Up until about a decade ago Marin still believed that her father had abandoned us. The fact that she never dug deeper into where he had gone I attributed to her love for me, her desire to protect me from the old wounds. But as she got older, she began to crave some sort of closure, and that's when I finally told her that the reiteration had gone wrong, that her father hadn't disappeared willfully but rather as the result of an accident.

Mom, I think I knew but didn't want to admit it to myself, she'd said.

I remember the day so well. I'd been helping her move into her new apartment in Cleveland, where she was adjuncting as a creative-writing instructor, and she plopped down on the futon and clasped her wrist over her head like she always did when she was nervous. She had started doing this in junior high, when her hearing loss was at its worst, before the implants helped restore her hearing a little bit.

How did you know?"I asked, touching the side of my forehead.

Sure, Dad was going through some things back then, but he wouldn't just leave without saying goodbye. No note? No e-mail? No phone call? It never made sense. But I had no other explanation so I accepted it, even though I didn't believe it.

She always made a clapping sound with believe—it was one of her many little signing signatures, and in fact she'd a written a poem about it, about how the sign for believe"was a combination of think and marry. She looked stunning in her bleached-blond hair and black leather and it caught my breath that this was actually my daughter, that I'd given birth to this remarkable creature who was now creating her own stories in the form of poems.

In a way that I hadn't anticipated, it was easier for Marin to accept that David's leaving was the result of a terrible accident involving the reiterations, maybe because this felt closer to a real accident, like a car crash.

So how did it go wrong? she asked me.

How could I tell her that I was how it went wrong? That I had fogged one of the delicate Mead-Fancher lenses in such a way that erased David? That I hadn't even had a chance to say a proper goodbye because I dreaded arousing his suspicion? That at the dark heart of all this was my own playwriting? Although Marin, as a child, couldn't have known this, David wanted to eliminate Lisa 2 for one reason only: he believed it was somehow responsible for the change in my writing and, by extension me. It's true that all my plays up to the Lisa 2 discovery had been of a certain type, stories that, when you boiled everything else away, were family dramas. If there were elements of horror, they were around the edges, in the shadows, *subtextual*, as my editor would say. Was David right that my switch to outright horror was connected to composing on Lisa 2? And was he right that as the tone of my writing changed, the tone of me changed as well? Was I morphing into some other version of myself, some other genre, parallel to my literary-genre switch?

19.

It's opening night and at the afterglow event in the garden behind the theatre my colleagues and students are mingling, enjoying hors d'oeuvres and cherry bourbon in honor of the play's northern-Michigan setting. Marin is here, in a yellow sundress and black lace-up boots and Aunt Elle's vintage drop earrings and her flaming blond hair. *Alice Doesn't* played funnier than I had expected, but also more terrifying, and more than one of my students has come up to me grinning with a maraschino cherry between her fingers, which at least assures me they were not drifting off during the castration scene.

It's a one-two punch, a perfect weekend. Tomorrow afternoon Marin reads her poems just around the corner at the Rathskeller, the campus coffee shop with its makeshift stage and framed posters of some of the authors who've read there over the years. Her new collection is coming out next spring and she hasn't shared any of the poems with me yet. They're about David, I think, and maybe me and us, the family we once were, and she's already cautioned me to remember my own mantra that not all writing is autobiographical. I think I must have first shared this theory with her when she was in ninth grade and she'd read one of my plays all the way through for the first time.

God, Mom, she had said, I didn't know you had a thing for Mr. Carlson.

One of the things David got right about Marin was her freckles. She still has them and although they're more subdued, they do still glow a bit when she gets an idea into her head that she can't let go of. Mr. Carlson was Marin's music teacher and I had used a slightly altered version of his name. In the play he and Lina have an affair that sets in motion the school scandal that's at the heart of the story and I wanted Marin to read it because she was starting to write poetry and I know it had taken me far too long as a writer to free myself from the fear that people—especially friends and family—would read my plays as autobiography.

I don't have a thing for Mr. Carlson, I told her. " wrote the play as a writer, not as your mother.

This was an exaggeration of course, but I wanted to make a point. And now, on the verge of her reading, it was coming back to haunt me. Would I be able to see myself in Marin's poems while at the same time understanding that I'd been created not by Marin the daughter but by Marin the writer?

I needn't have worried. On the stage, in her lucky navy-blue coverall, she shined and, in her shining, her poems shined. The tables lifted, the walls disappeared, the sun shined through the open roof, the coyotes howled in the distance as she read:

I don't remember how it is I've come to know that Mom isn't Mom

That's my Marin, always detecting the truth where no one else can.

The Lisa is putting everything away before turning off.

To terminate the operation, hold down the Apple key while you type a period.

WARNING: If you intend to turn the disk off, wait until the light in the Lisa's on-off button goes off.

Acknowledgements

Thank you to Derek White for believing in *Lisa 2, v1.0* and for bringing her to life. Thank you to Derek and Garielle Lutz for careful reading and for edits that make this book the best version of itself. For making space in *3:AM Magazine* for my writing over the years, thank you to Andrew Gallix. Thank you to Cal Freeman. I'm grateful to my colleagues at the University of Detroit Mercy for not blinking an eye when I've published books that go off the rails. This book is for Maddy, Niko, Chandler, Ali, and Sheri. This book is for Lisa 1.

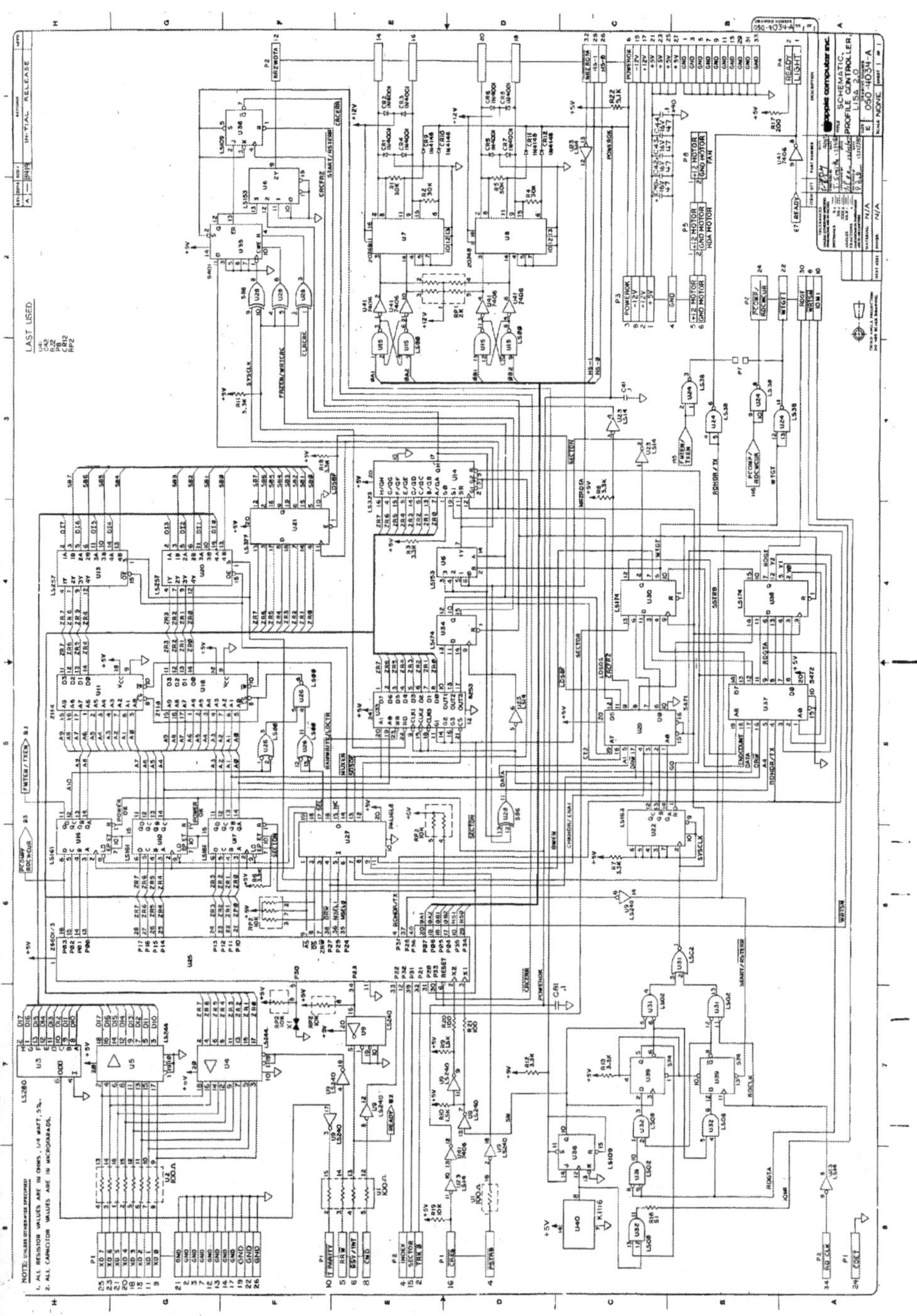
SCHEMATIC, PROFILE CONTROLLER LISA 2.0
050-4034-A
INITIAL RELEASE
LAST USED
NOTE: UNLESS OTHERWISE SPECIFIED
1. ALL RESISTOR VALUES ARE IN OHMS, 1/4 WATT, 5%.
2. ALL CAPACITOR VALUES ARE IN MICROFARADS.

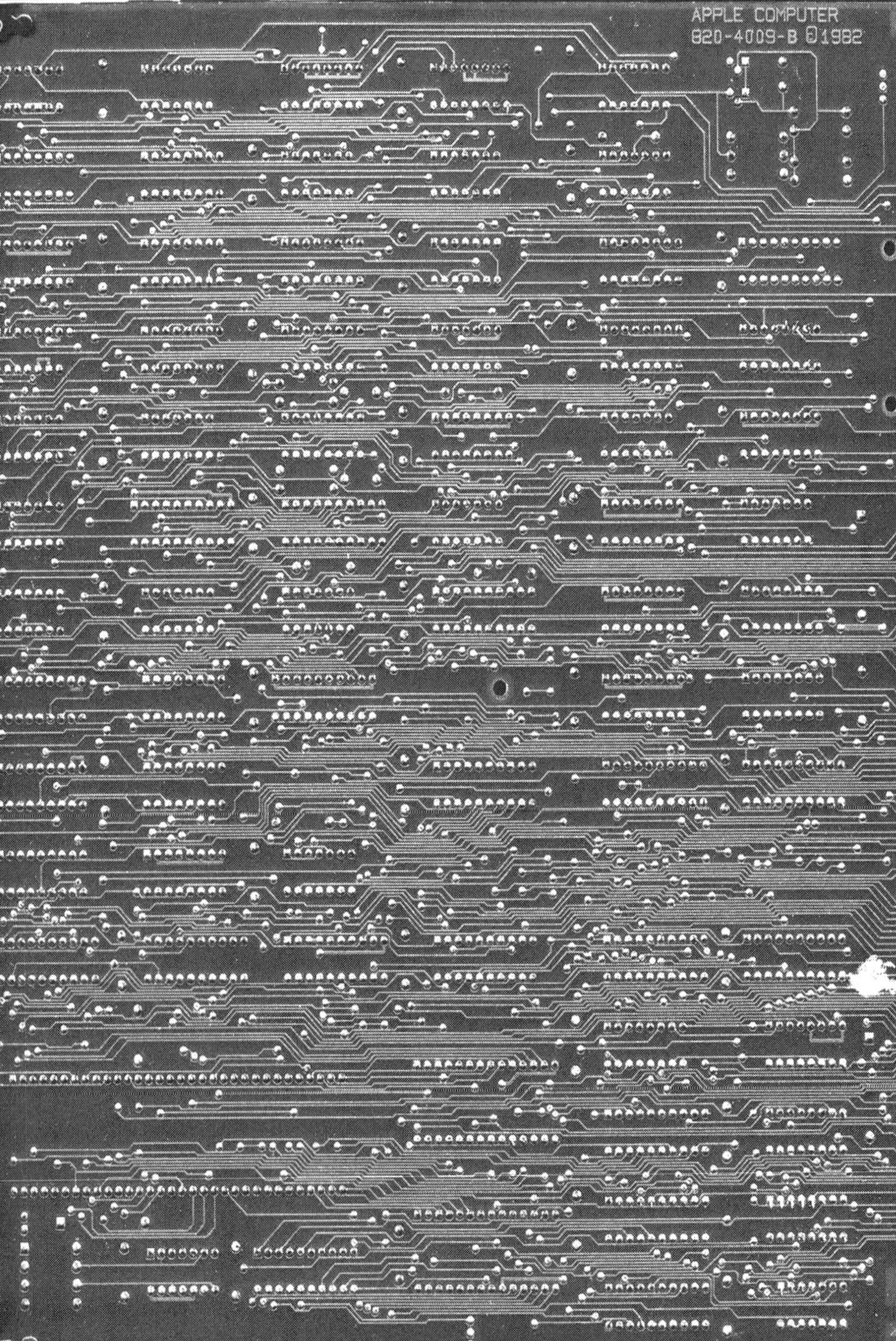
APPLE COMPUTER
820-4009-B ©1982

Made in the USA
Middletown, DE
24 January 2025

69868094R00084